Anna Cora Ogden Mowatt Ritchie

Italian Life and Legends

Anna Cora Ogden Mowatt Ritchie

Italian Life and Legends

ISBN/EAN: 9783337393212

Printed in Europe, USA, Canada, Australia, Japan

Cover: Foto ©Andreas Hilbeck / pixelio.de

More available books at **www.hansebooks.com**

ITALIAN

LIFE AND LEGENDS.

BY

ANNA CORA ("MOWATT") RITCHIE,

AUTHOR OF

"FAIRY FINGERS," "MUTE SINGER," "CLERGYMAN'S WIFE," "MIMIC LIFE," TWIN
ROSES," AUTOBIOGRAPHY OF AN ACTRESS," ETC.

WITH ILLUSTRATIONS.

NEW YORK:

Carleton, Publisher, Madison Square.

LONDON: S. LOW, SON & CO.

MDCCCLXX.

PREFACE.

In presenting to the public "Italian Life and Legends," I cannot but believe that the many friends of my sister, Mrs. Ritchie, will welcome with interest another volume from her pen — that pen which is now laid at rest, and never more can speak to us in tones of sympathy and love.

The sketches were written during the author's residence in Italy, for the most part in Florence, in the years 1864 and 1865. A few appeared in periodicals at the time they were written; others have never before been published. They are now offered to the public because it is believed that the historic incidents they contain, together with the wild romance of Italian character, claim a decided interest.

M. G. T.

New York, Nov. 1, 1870.

CONTENTS.

	Page
SAVONAROLA	9
VITTORIA COLONNA	53
GALILEO'S VILLA	71
CONVENT OF VALLOMBROSA	94
BRIDGES OF FLORENCE	107
DANTE	118
FLORENTINE FEUDS	133
FEUDS BETWEEN THE BIANCHI AND NERI	145
THE VILLAGE SERRAVEZZA	157
THE PROTESTANT CEMETERY AT FLORENCE	169

Mrs. Browning — Dr. Southwood Smith — Mrs. Frances Trollope, and other Celebrities.

| OVERFLOW OF ARNO — ARTIST, AND THE STORY OF A MAD SINGER | 180 |
| FEDI THE SCULPTOR | 191 |

CONTENTS.

	Page
ADELAIDE RISTORI, AND PICCOLOMINI	200
THE BEAUTIFUL HORROR. A FLORENTINE LEGEND	211
GINEVRA	227
LA BELLE CLEMENTINE	241
CATERINA SFORZA	268

Thrice Wedded, thrice Widowed. An Italian Chatelaine.

ITALIAN LIFE AND LEGENDS.

SAVONAROLA.

THE Piazza della Signoria is situated in the most central part of Florence, faced by the grand Palazzo Vecchio, and enriched by marvels of art from the hands of Michel Angelo, John of Bologna, Ammanato, Orgagna, etc.; but it is not on account of its felicitous locality, or its world-renowned surroundings alone, that this Piazza is celebrated. It is consecrated by historic associations which might well stir with enthusiasm the most sluggish and insensible natures. Among the heart-rending human tragedies that have been enacted upon that gayly beautiful Piazza, was the cruel martyrdom of the pure-minded, truth-devoted Savonarola and his two friends. For more than three centuries—that is, from the time of his death in 1498, until within about the last thirty years—this Piazza, on the anniversary of that merciless sacrifice, was strewed with fresh violets, in grateful remembrance of the good he achieved and the wrong he endured. Mrs.

Browning thus alludes to this touching custom, and to the tardy recognition of his manifold benefactions to Florence:

> " All the Winters that have snowed,
> Cannot snow out the scent from stone and air
>   Of a sincere man's virtues. . . .
> . . . . It were foul
>   To grudge Savonarola and the rest
> Their violets! rather pay them quick and fresh.
>   The emphasis of death makes manifest
> The eloquence of action in our flesh,
>   And men who, living, were but dimly guessed,
> When once free from their life's entangled mesh,
>   Show their full length in graves."

It is singular that no complete and satisfactory biography of so remarkable a man as Savonarola existed, until Professor Villari, of Florence, some four or five years ago, published his " Life and Times of Savonarola." This able author devoted ten years to incessant researches in the careful preparation of his work. Its vigorously impressive style, its minute details, and the authenticity of the information given, cannot be too highly estimated. About a year after Signor Villari's book was published, " Romola " appeared. Savonarola is made one of the heroes of that brilliant novel.

Girolamo Savonarola was born at Ferrara, on the 21st of September, 1452. His youth was meditative, studious, and uneventful, until he reached his twentieth year. At that time a member of the ancient Strozzi family, who had been banished from Florence, resided at Ferrara, in the neighborhood of Savonarola's paternal home. The illustrious Florentine had a beautiful but illegitimate daughter. The youthful Savonarola was kindly received by the Strozzi, and, being thrown in contact with the fair maiden, became deeply enamored. The cordiality of her greetings, and the pleasure she appeared to take in his visits, led Savonarola into a serious error. Not for a moment doubting that she reciprocated his attachment, he confidently solicited her hand. Her haughty reply at once amazed and crushed him. She answered proudly that a *Strozzi* could not wed a *Savonarola!* Without remonstrance or reproach, Savonarola withdrew; but from that time he became subject to fits of deep melancholy. This was his first affection; and we may judge of its strength by its constancy, for it was his last.

While his mind was still in a very dejected state, he was strongly impressed by the preaching of a Dominican friar, who visited Ferrara. Savonarola's thoughts soon turned wholly away from the world. At the age of twenty-three, he visited Bologna, and entered the convent of St. Dominic. He stated that the gross corruption of the age was the cause of his retirement.

His monastic life was characterized by great devoutness, the rude simplicity of his habits, and the exalted state of his mind. He hardly ate enough to support nature. His bed was of wicker-work, with a sack of straw and a blanket. He had frequent trances, and often gave vent to his thoughts and emotions in poetry.

When war threatened Ferrara, the superior of the convent sought a less uncertain shelter for some of the brotherhood. Savonarola was sent to Florence. There he entered that Convent of St. Mark in which he afterward effected reforms destined to become so important a feature in secular as well as ecclesiastical history.

At this period Lorenzo the Magnificent reigned in all his superb licentiousness over Florence. Its inhabitants, nobles and populace, rich and poor, were alike immersed in a sea of profligate gayety. *Fêtes*, dances, tournaments, unchaste orgies, drunken revels, and lower depravities, wholly engrossed the public mind. Lorenzo was a patron of the fine arts, a man of letters, an author, and had no mean gift of poetry; yet he could debase himself by composing obscene ballads, to be sung during carnivals by young noblemen, who, dressed as devils, ran shouting, yelling, and singing, through the streets. Villari declares that these ballads are so revoltingly indecent, that in the present day they would not be tolerated by the most depraved taste.

Savonarola was horror-stricken by the profane boldness of the unscrupulous potentate, who only employed his rich mental attributes, and the power conferred by his princely office, to debase or oppress his subjects. Holy promptings clamored incessantly within the pious friar's spirit, and urged him to rise up and counteract Lorenzo's baneful influence.

It was one of Savonarola's most striking characteristics, that whenever he saw there was a good work to be done, he always felt that he was the man called to do it; and he had perfect faith in his own strength to accomplish any task to which he set his hand.

This determination to wage war against the unbridled license which ran riot in Florence, was confirmed by a remarkable vision. The heavens seemed opened to him; the future calamities of the Church were vividly represented, and he heard a voice which commanded him to declare to the people the misfortunes with which they were menaced. Up to this period, Savonarola's sermons had attracted little attention; but he now electrified his hearers by boldly denouncing Lorenzo, and the depravities of which he was the unblushing instigator.

This sermon caused five of the principal citizens of Florence to visit Savonarola, and bid him beware. Savonarola told them that he was the mouthpiece of the Lord, which man could not silence. They

threatened him with banishment. Stirred by a
prophetic spirit, he answered, "I am a stranger, and
Lorenzo is not only a citizen, but the first of citizens;
yet it is I who will remain, and he who shall leave
the city."

His visions now became more and more frequent,
and more absorbing. They invariably formed the
subject of his sermons. At times he resolved not to
preach what had been revealed to him during these
visions; but when he entered the pulpit he found
himself powerless to resist his spiritual promptings
—his own volition had no command over his utter-
ances. Sometimes, while preaching, he fell into a
state of trance or ecstasy.

Multitudes flocked to hear him, and were stirred
to remorse by his bold denunciations of crime. His
voice had remarkable power, and historians dwell
upon its tones of thunder; but it had also a pleading pathos, and the softness which corresponded to
his merciful nature. He exerted a magnetic influence over his hearers, which melted to devotion even
those who came to scoff.

Villari says: "It would be impossible to give an
idea of the force of his expressions, of the vividness
of his descriptions, of the works of his imagination,
of the confidence of his faith that his visions came
from heaven. He repeated the words he had heard

pronounced by invisible beings; his deep and solemn voice was re-echoed from the vaulted roofs of the Temple; it descended like a divine manifestation on the people, who were roused to a state of ecstasy, and who trembled with terror, wonder, and delight."

In 1490 he was chosen Prior of the Convent of St. Mark. It was customary for a Prior, upon his election, to pay homage to Lorenzo the Magnificent. Savonarola refused to comply with this observance. He said that his election came from God alone, and that to him alone he rendered obeisance. Lorenzo tried to conciliate him; he went to mass at St. Mark's, and then walked in the gardens of the convent. Savonarola quietly pursued his studies, and the Magnificent waited in vain to be joined by the humble friar.

When Lorenzo was stricken with a mortal illness, and his last hours approached, he desired to see Savonarola, and to receive absolution at his hands. "I know no honest friar but him!" was the dying magnate's exclamation. Savonarola promply obeyed the summons. Lorenzo told him that there was three especial sins which he wished to confess: the sacking of Volterra, the money pillaged at the Monte delle Fanciulle which had caused so many deaths, and the bloodshed after the conspiracy of the

Pazzi. Savonarola bade him restore all he had un-justly taken, or order his sons to restore it, and told him that he must have a lively faith in the mercy of God. Lorenzo affirmed that he had that faith, and reluctantly promised to return whatever he had taken unlawfully. Then Savonarola impressively declared to him that there was one thing more to be done. "You must restore liberty to the people of Florence!" exclaimed the friar. Lorenzo, with one last effort, raised himself in his bed, and scornfully turned his back, without speaking. Savonarola left him, and the Magnificent died a prey to the most cruel mental torture (8th April, 1492).

Mrs. Browning makes mention of this incident in her "Casa Guidi Windows:"

> "Who also by a princely deathbed cried,
>   'Loose Florence, or God will not loose thy soul,'
> While the Magnificent fell back and died
>   Beneath the star-looks, shooting from the cowl,
> Which turned to wormwood bitterness the wide
>   Deep sea of his ambition."

In that year Savonarola had a dream which he believed to be a divine revelation. He saw in the sky a hand holding a drawn sword; upon the sword was written, "The sword of the Lord on the earth, and speedily." Suddenly the sword turned toward the earth, the air became dark, showers of swords and arrows and fire descended, and fearful thunders were heard, while the whole earth became a prey to wars, famines, and pestilences. This vision was afterward represented by a large number of engravings, and upon numerous medals.

After Savonarola became Prior he commenced his reforms in the Convent of St. Mark. He fitted the monks to live by their own labor — formed schools in which they were taught painting, sculpture, architecture, and the art of copying and illuminating manuscripts. He made the three especial objects of study theology, morals, and the Holy Scriptures; that the latter might be better comprehended, the brethren were instructed in Greek, Hebrew, and the Oriental languages.

Savonarola predicted the coming of the French army, "of a new Cyrus, who would traverse Italy as a conqueror, without meeting with any resistance or breaking a single lance." Italy was at that time wholly unprotected. When the news suddenly arrived that the French troops were crossing the Alps, she had no national armies and no friendly foreign forces. The terrified Florentines rushed to Savonarola, by whom the coming of the foe had been predicted, and implored his aid and counsel. Crowds thronged the streets in a state of wild disorder. Soon the popular fury turned against Piero de' Medici (who had succeeded his father Lorenzo, and had surpassed him in the magnitude of his crimes), and against the nobles and wealthy citizens. Not only were their houses in danger of being sacked and burned, but their lives were in jeopardy.

At this crisis Savonarola mounted the pulpit of the Duomo. The church was crammed with people, rudely armed to defend themselves against the invaders. Savonarola commenced his discourse with these words: "Behold, the sword *has* descended, the scourges have commenced, the prophecies are being fulfilled!" So irresistible was his eloquence, that the passions of the multitude were calmed, and no violence was committed that day. Historians ascribe this fact entirely to the ascendancy which he had acquired over the minds of the people.

At the meeting of the Signoria, who assembled to discuss the steps to be taken, Piero de' Medici was pronounced incapable of ruling the republic, and it was resolved that ambassadors should be sent to the French King Charles, and that Savonarola should accompany them.

The chosen ambassadors set out, the next day, in their splendid equipages; Savonarola followed on foot. The ambassadors were coldly received by the King, who refused to treat with them. Then Savonarola entered the French camp alone, and stood before the King, as he sat among his generals. The friar addressed the sovereign in a fearless tone,

and told him that the Lord had sent him to deliver
Italy from her afflictions, and that if he forgot the
work of the Lord, another hand would be selected for
its accomplishment. The King listened with profound respect, and gave Savonarola the assurance of
his friendly intentions.

Meantime, Piero de' Medeci, after a vain attempt
to resist by force of arms, fled from Florence.

After much difficulty and procrastination, King
Charles signed a treaty with the Florentines, but
delayed his departure from Florence. His soldiers
filled the city, creating daily scenes of riot and confusion; robberies and murders were frequent; the
citizens were defenceless and in despair — still the
King could not be persuaded to leave. Once more
Savonarola was called upon to appear before the
King. The result of this interview was a speedy
withdrawal of Charles and his army; but not until
his retainers had sacked the splendid palace which
had been appropriated to his use. Through this
barefaced robbery a large portion of the valuable
collections of the Medici passed into the hands of
the French.

The Florentines now turned more confidently than
ever to Savonarola. They owed their freedom to
him; his counsels alone could be trusted; his prophecies had been fulfilled; he alone had been able to

influence the King and relieve Florence from the
heavy incubus of the royal presence. Villari says:
"The man, therefore, who was destined to save the
people of Florence was Friar Girolamo Savonarola;
the hour had struck when he was to enter into
public life; events had carried him forward irresistibly in that direction, notwithstanding the firmness
with which he had hitherto held back."

From the pulpit of the Duomo, Savonarola told
his hearers boldly that the reform in Florence must
begin with things *spiritual;* that the people must
purify their minds, renounce their evil courses, and
abstain from all profligacy and profanity, and thus
they might fit themselves to construct a new government. He set forth that the groundwork of that
government ought to be, "that no individual should
have any benefit but what is general, and the people
alone must have the power of choosing the magistrates and of approving the laws."

Speaking of the successful formation of this new
government, planned by Savonarola, Villari says:
"And all this occurred in a brief space of time,
without a sword having been drawn, without a drop
of blood having been shed, without a single civil
riot, and that, too, in Florence, the city of tumults.
But the greatest marvel of all was the power exer-
cised by a single man, and he a simple friar, direct-

ing the work from his pulpit, and bringing it to a happy conclusion ; an instance unexampled in history of the omnipotence of the human will and of persuasive eloquence. He was never to be seen at meetings in the Piazza, nor at the sittings of the Signoria, but he became the very soul of the whole people, and the chief author of all the laws by which the new government was constituted."

Villari thus describes the total change which took place in the whole city: "The women gave up their rich ornaments — dressed with simplicity and walked demurely; the young men became, as if by enchantment, modest and religious; instead of carnival songs, religious hymns were chanted. During the hours of mid-day rest the tradesmen were seen seated in their shops reading the Bible or some work of the friar; habits of prayers were resumed, the churches were well attended, and alms were freely given. But the most wonderful thing of all was to find bankers and merchants refunding, from scruples of conscience, sums of money, amounting sometimes to thousands of florins, which they had unrighteously acquired."

But this state of unwonted and happy quietude was of brief duration. The unstable and unprincipled Charles the Eighth broke faith with the Florentines, and violated every promise he had given.

The city was in great danger, for Piero de' Medici was making mighty efforts to return, and reassume his despotic sway. He had obtained the favor of the French King, and was even now approaching the city in his company.

To rescue the republic from peril so imminent, Savonarola was, for the third time, sent to the King. The sovereign and friar met at Poggibonsi. Again Savonarola warned the King that his perfidy would draw down divine retribution. Awed by that menace, Charles once more gave solemn pledges — which, however, were never redeemed.

Savonarola, with all the potency of his powerful rhetoric, opposed the return of the Medici, and the reëstablishment of despotism. Piero de' Medici was eventually driven back, and took refuge in Rome.

On the death of Pope Innocent the Eighth, Cardinal Rodrigo Borgia, father of the infamous Lucretia Borgia, became Pope Alexander the Sixth. Crime, in its lowest, widest, blackest form, sat unveiled and triumphant on the Papal throne. Who can wonder that Pope Borgia was Savonarola's bitterest enemy? Savonarola had addressed him a respectful, yet daring letter of remonstrance, setting forth the injuries done to the Church by the immoral lives of her Popes. A man like Borgia was

not likely to pardon such a rebuke. In 1495 the
Pope invited Savonarola to Rome, but his friends,
who had learned that Borgia favored a conspiracy
against the upright friar, entreated him not to obey
the summons. They assured him it was only a
snare laid for his imprisonment or assassination.
Fortunately, a severe internal malady, which rendered travelling impossible, afforded him a legiti-
mate excuse for delay. Already his life had been
several times attempted. Even in the city he could
not venture forth without an armed escort.

Savonarola's excuses were seemingly accepted by
the Pope, but before long the friar was again commanded, and more peremptorily than before, to
hasten to Rome, and was suspended from preaching.

Savonarola refused to leave Florence, but he was
silenced. Fra Domenico, his zealous and devoted
friend, preached in his stead and promulgated his
doctrines; but they lacked the influence of Savonarola's personal presence and overwhelming eloquence.

Savonarola's active mind and his love of usefulness compelled him to engage in good works which
might be effected out of the pulpit. The carnival
of 1496 was approaching, and the obscene orgies
which the Medici had inaugurated were still in

vogue; even the children took a prominent part in festivities at which all decency was ignored.

One of the favorite amusements was to light bonfires in the Piazza della Signoria, and dance around them, singing lascivious ballads, and then to conclude by a game of throwing stones. This brutal game invariably maimed, and often killed, people who were passing in the streets.

Savonarola undertook what he modestly called "The Children's Reform." He gave a new direction to their amusements, and endeavored to substitute religious, for carnival or bacchanalian ceremonies.

The children were in the habit of forming themselves into bands of extempore robbers, and taking possession of much-frequented localities, to bar the passage of every one who walked that way, until the contents of his purse had been distributed among them. The money thus forcibly obtained was squandered in festivities and revelry. Savonarola had small altars set up in the localities where the children were accustomed to congregate, and he told them they might collect alms to distribute among the poor, but they should take no money by force, and waste none in carousing. He allowed them to sing, as before; but he taught them hymns, some of his own composition, which they were to substitute for their profane and disgusting Medici ballads. He instructed the good friar Domenico to collect the children, and allow them the pleasurable excitement of choosing from among themselves a leader, who was presented to the Signoria, and who made known to that body the object of the reform. The children were highly delighted at their own importance, and entered into the spirit of the good work with great zeal. The murderous game of stones was for the first time given up. The children collected three hundred ducats, which were given to the poor.

Savonarola's friends now made such earnest appeals to Pope Borgia, that he granted the friar permission to preach during Lent. The Pope, either to conciliate Savonarola, or because he feared him, or to lay another snare, offered him a cardinal's hat, on condition that he would change the style of language he had been accustomed to use in his sermons. Savonarola quietly refused the conditions, and the new dignity.

During his Lent preachings, the multitudes which flocked to hear him were so great, that a lofty amphitheatre, rising to the first row of windows, was erected in the inside of the Duomo. This amphitheatre had seventeen small steps, on which the children were seated. Savonarola often addressed

them, for to them he looked for the future regener-
ation of Florence.

The attempts upon his life became so open, that
he had to be conducted to the Duomo by armed
friends. And they reëscorted him to the convent,
without venturing to leave him for a moment un-
surrounded. These Lent discourses are chronicled
as the most bold and the most impressive which he
ever delivered. The historian says : " His sermons
are to the Florentine history of this brief period,
what the orations of Demosthenes are to that of
Athens, of Cicero to that of Rome."

It often happened that the princes of Italy wrote
to Savonarola, to remonstrate with him, because
they imagined that *they* were the persons alluded
to in his sermons.

Savonarola was again ordered by the Pope to abstain from all preaching, in public or in private, and
commanded to acknowledge the authority of the
Vicar General of the Lombard congregation, and
to proceed to whatever place he appointed. Pope
Borgia knew that if Savonarola were to leave the
Tuscan territory, he would immediately be in his
power. Savonarola saw through the plot, and at
once made up his mind not to obey ; but he sent a
conciliatory answer to the Pope, giving his reasons.
The Pope once more pretended to be satisfied, and

resorted to cajolery; still, however, commanding Savonarola to abstain from preaching.

At this period, Florence was in a state of great misery. She was threatened with famine, and the plague had broken out, and was making daily progress. The people were almost starving, and in despair, without any prospect of succor. As usual, they turned to Savonarola for comfort and counsel. The Signoria implored him to break the silence wrongfully imposed by the Pope. Savonarola, greatly moved by the deplorable state of the city, yielded to the solicitations of the chief magistrates, and returned without permission to the pulpit. So long as the Florentines could hear his voice, they gained courage to face any calamity.

It was a singular coincidence, that Savonarola had hardly preached his sermon of consolation, conjuring his hearers to give up their vices, and lead good lives, that they might receive the blessings of Heaven, when the long hoped-for supply of men and of wheat arrived from Marseilles. All Florence was frantic with joy, and the people's confidence in Savonarola was redoubled by this incident. The bells rang out a joyful peal, artillery was discharged, and thanksgivings were offered up in all the churches.

When the carnival season of another year, 1497,

approached, the Arrabbiati, which was the party violently opposed to Savonarola, again made preparations for the "scandalous feast of the Medici," and for the game of stones, which Savonarola had prevented on the previous year. But Savonarola, aided by his well-tried friend, Fra Domenico, invented a ceremony which would better occupy the hands and minds of the little people — this was the making of a bonfire of vanities. The children, under the direction of their young leader, were instructed to march through the city in white robes, with olive crowns on their heads, and knock at every door to gather voluntary contributions for the bonfire. They were to ask for objects which came under the head of vanities or the Anathema. These were obscene pictures, portraits of females of bad repute, immodest and immoral books, carnival masks and dresses, artificial accessories of the toilet, tapestries with unchaste designs, cards, dice, gaming boards, etc. On receiving the Anathema, the children repeated a prayer taught them by Savonarola, and went on their way. On the last day of the Carnival, the articles collected were carried by the juvenile reformers to the Piazza della Signoria.

The children marched in solemn procession, bearing their unhallowed burdens. Before them was borne a statue of the infant Saviour, the exquisite work of Donatelli, supported by four angels. Jesus pointed, with the left hand, to a crown of thorns; the right hand was stretched out in the act of blessing the people. A dense crowd, holding red crosses and olive branches, and singing hymns, accompanied the children. On the piazza, an octangular pyramid had been formed, 60 feet in height, and 240 feet in circumference at its base; it was divided into fifteen stages, and on these the vanities were heaped. The interior of the pyramid was filled with combustible materials, and on the top was a monstrous image representing the carnival. While the children sang, denouncing carnival vices, the pile was set on fire. The great bell of the Palazzo Vecchio was tolled, and the multitude shouted for joy.

Savonarola has been severely reprehended by the writers of after times, because it is supposed that many valuable manuscripts and rare books, and even works of art, were destroyed in that bonfire; but there is no proof that such was the case, and Savonarola's love and admiration for the fine arts cannot be questioned. The most eminent artists of the age were his devoted friends. Michael Angelo was constantly seen in the Duomo, when Savonarola preached, and continued to read his sermons with delight, even in old age.

In the second part will be traced the fall of Savonarola from his wonderful moral autocracy of Florence, until he was burned at the stake in the public square of the city.

PART II.

Upon Ascension Day of that year, the party opposed to Savonarola conspired to have his pulpit blown up, by fireworks, while he was preaching. But this attempt was abandoned, for fear of injury to the congregation. The Arrabbiati then scattered all sorts of filth in the pulpit, and drove sharp spikes in the places where Savonarola, in the warmth of his discourse, often struck his hands. The object of these conspirators was to raise a commotion, in the hope that an opportunity to slay Savonarola would occur.

The Piagnoni, a party full of gentle piety, who were friendly to Savonarola, went to the Duomo at break of day, and cleansed the pulpit and removed the spikes.

Savonarola, surrounded by his armed escort, reached the Duomo in safety, and commenced his sermon. Suddenly, while he was preaching, a tremendous crash was heard, the alms-chest was thrown down, drums were beaten, benches were torn up and tossed about, and the doors flung open. The Compagnacci (evil companions) with the Arrabbiati had raised this alarming tumult. In the midst of this confusion, two of the Otto (eight rulers), who thought that the dignity of their office rendered their persons secure, rushed forward to kill Savonarola, but his friends had already formed a circle about him and barred all approach. They conducted him triumphantly through the crowd, back to the Convent of St. Mark.

Pope Borgia now sent his long-threatened letter of excommunication, in which every one who would not incur the like penalty was prohibited from rendering the friar any assistance, or having any communication with him.

Savonarola wrote a letter declaring the excommunication to be invalid, as it was based upon false charges, invented by enemies.

Villari says that the effect of this excommunication, which was solemnly read in the cathedral, was that " profligacy was established as if by incantation; the churches were empty, the taverns full; women come forth wearing indecent dresses, and their hitherto hidden jewels; perfumed youths went about singing carnival songs under the windows of their mistresses, who no longer blushed when hearing them. In less than one month the days of Lorenzo the Magnificent seemed to have come back, and all thoughts of patriotism and liberty were forgotten."

Meantime the plague had again broken out, and Savonarola was one of the most zealous and untiring of the small band who had the strength or courage to minister to the stricken.

When Christmas day arrived, his friends entreated him to ascend the pulpit once more. He yielded, and celebrated three masses upon that day at St. Mark, and the first Sunday in Lent (February, 1498) again appeared in the pulpit of the Duomo; the Archbishop of Florence, Leonardo de' Medici, threatened to withhold the communion and burial in consecrated ground from any one who was present at Savonarola's discourse. But the Signoria showed their resentment by intimating to the Archbishop that he must resign his office within two hours, or he would be declared to be a rebel.

This year there was a second bonfire of vanities, upon the Piazza della Signoria, in spite of the violent opposition of the Compagnacci. The Pyramid was surmounted by a figure of Lucifer, surrounded by representations of the seven mortal sins. The conflagration was even greater than on the previous year.

After this the Pope wrote a violent letter to the Signoria, threatening to excommunicate the whole city if Savonarola, was permitted to preach. The Signoria (the officers of which were changed every two months) had no alternative, and sent an order to Savonarola requesting him to deliver no more sermons. The next day, which was the third Sunday in Lent, he took an affectionate leave of the people, informing them of the order he had received.

About this time a singular event took place, which suddenly turned the capricious current of public opinion against Savonarola. Francesco di Puglia, preaching in the Church of the Santo Spirito, denounced Savonarola's doctrines as heretical, and challenged him to the Ordeal by Fire, affirming that if Savonarola were truly a servant of the Lord, a miracle would certainly be wrought in his behalf, and he would issue from the flames unharmed; but if he were burned, his impostures would be made manifest, and the people would be awakened from their pernicious delusion. The Franciscan monk asserted that he was prepared to perish himself for the sake of putting Savonarola to the test.

Savonarola, to the surprise and dismay of his adherents, refused the challenge. IIe replied that he had other work to do, and that he did not feel himself called upon to undergo this ordeal. But when Savonarola declined, his heroic friend, Fra Domenico — who was gifted with a stolid fortitude which defied physical pain — rose up, and boldly accepted the challenge. Savonarola rebuked him, and argued with him — in vain. At last, seeing his unflinching resolution, and perfect faith in the triumph that awaited him, the conviction was forced upon Savonarola that Fra Domenico must be acting under the promptings of inspiration, and that the Lord would guard him through the fire.

The Franciscan monk, who evidently had anticipated Savonarola's refusal, rejected Fra Domenico as a substitute, and proclaimed that he would only undergo the ordeal with Savonarola. But Fra Domenico was resolved, and the Signoria felt bound to urge Francesco di Puglia to consent; for all the friars of St. Mark, and of the Dominican convent of Fiesole, had offered to pass through the fire, and had compelled Savonarola to make known their wishes to the Signoria, and to desire that body to select one of the Dominican order for every Minorite who would accept the challenge. The excitement rose to such a pitch that men, women, and even children, in crowds offered themselves as candidates to pass through the flames.

The 7th of April was fixed upon for the trial. Fra Giuliano Rondinelli was accepted to accompany Fra Domenico. Francesco di Puglia, who had given the challenge, held himself in readiness, he said, to enter the flames with Savonarola, but with him only. The city was in a state of frenzied enthusiasm to witness the proposed spectacle. Upon the famous Piazza della Signoria lay the pile of fagots — wood sprinkled with gunpowder, oil, and resinous substances. It was eight feet long, ten feet wide at the base, and five feet high. In the middle was a passage two feet wide, through which the champions were to pass.

When the mace-bearers of the Signoria announced that the hour for the trial had arrived, the friars of St. Mark immediately went forth in procession. Fra Domenico walked between his brethren, Malatesta Sacramoro and Francesco Salviati. He was perfectly confident, and eager for the test. He wore a bright red velvet cape, and carried a tall cross. Savonarola followed him in a white robe, bearing the sacrament. The Piazza was thronged, and the windows, balconies, and roofs of the surrounding houses perilously crowded.

A body of three hundred infantry had been stationed in front of the Loggia de Lanzi, commanded by Marcuccio Salviati, a faithful adherent of Savonarola. But there were also five hundred Compagnacci, Savonarola's bitterest foes, under the leadership of the brutal Dolfo Spini, and five hundred of the infantry of the Signoria stationed in front of the palace. Thus there were a thousand armed men, masters of the Piazza, all ready to offer any indignity to Savonarola, or even to do him any personal injury.

The monks of St. Mark had taken their appointed places, but Francesco di Puglia and Giuliano Rondinelli had not yet made their appearance. They were in the palace, holding a secret conference with the Signoria. The Minorite friars now began to invent causes for delay, and, if possible, to raise up obstacles to the ordeal. They ordered the Director of the ordeal to say that the red cape of Fra Domenico might have been charmed by Savonarola, and must be removed. Fra Domenico at once took off the suspected cape. Then the Minorites said that his gown might have been charmed. Fra Domenico willingly consented to lay it aside. He was taken into the palace, and put on the dress of the Dominican, Alessandro Strozzi. After this the Minorites would not allow him near Savonarola, expressing a fear that the latter might renew his incantations.

The crowd, which had been waiting, eagerly expectant, for many hours, now became impatient at the delay, and their murmurs soon broke out into a tumult. The Arrabbiati had agreed among themselves that they would take advantage of any disorder to seize Savonarola and put him to death. They made the attempt, but Salviati kept his soldiers close before the Loggia, and drawing a line on the ground with his sword, cried out, "Whoever passes this line will find what the weapon of Marcuccio Salviati can do!"

Order was hardly restored when a violent storm of thunder and lightning broke over the heads of the people, and threatened to put an end to the trial. But the populace were too pertinaciously determined to behold the spectacle to stir from their places. They remained unmoved until the pouring rain unexpectedly ceased.

The Minorites now requested that Fra Domenico would lay down the crucifix he held in his hand. He complied, and Savonarola substituted the Sacrament. The Minorites violently protested; to bear the consecrated host into the flames would be sacrilege, and could not be permitted. Savonarola and Fra Domenico refused to yield this point, and an argument arose between them and the Minorite friars, who were rejoiced at the delay. The Signoria took advantage of this dispute to order that the trial should not take place.

The populace were thrown into a state of indignant fury and disappointment, and turned their wrath upon Savonarola. Even his own party maintained that, others failing, *he* ought to have walked alone through the fire, and miraculously exhibited his supernatural powers. His enemies openly accused him of cowardice, and of having been proved an impostor. Friends and foes wanted to see a miracle; they *would have* a miracle; and if Savonarola were a man of God, a miracle must be wrought in his person! But for the brave soldiers of the noble Salviati, who, with their drawn swords, defended Savonarola and Fra Domenico against the enraged mob, they would not have reached the Convent of St. Mark alive.

Savonarola had worked no miracle! He had cheated his disciples out of the wondrous spectacle every heart palpitated to behold! From that hour he was torn from the pedestal to which popular love and gratitude had raised him. Who cared that the city had owed its freedom and its purification from the worst abuses to him? Or that he had taught the Florentines how to frame their new gov-

ernment? Or that when others fled from the pestilence he had tended the plague-stricken with never-
flagging devotion? Or that his voice had consoled
the starving, and kept alive their dying hopes when
gaunt Famine walked the streets? Or that he had
rescued this fair city from the depredations and
violence of the French army, and prevailed upon
the French King to take his departure? What
were all the friar's benefactions if he could work no
miracle — if he would not even trust his body to the
flames?

Not only did the Minorite friars consider themselves the victors, though their champion had not
even appeared upon the piazza, but the Signoria
awarded them an annual pension of sixty lire for
seventy years, "as a reward for the services they
had rendered."

The friars of the Convent of St. Mark could not
appear in the streets without being insulted, called
hypocrites and impostors, and having stones thrown
at them.

On the afternoon of Palm Sunday, the 8th of
April, the Convent of St. Mark was attacked by a
mob, headed by the Arrabbiati. The people who
were attending vespers in the church were assaulted
by a volley of stones. The church was rapidly
vacated and the doors of the convent barred. Sav-

onarola's small band of remaining friends, in number about thirty, stationed themselves within, to defend the convent. Foreseeing the danger, they had concealed weapons in a small chamber ·in the cloister, unknown to Savonarola. They armed sixteen of the friars, who presented a most singular appearance, with helmets on their heads, halberts in their hands, and cuirasses over their long Dominican gowns.

While the assailants were thundering at the doors, Savonarola implored his self-constituted defenders to lay down their arms, and proposed to give himself up without delay. Neither his secular friends nor the friars would listen to this suggestion. Soon the mace-bearers arrived with a proclamation from the Signoria, ordering every one in the convent to surrender, and announcing that Savonarola was banished, and must leave within twelve hours.

The · fury of the attacking party increased. They set fire to the doors, while some scaled the walls and got into the cloisters. They sacked the infirmary and the cells, and entered into the sacristy, breaking open the doors of the choir, where Savonarola and his followers were at prayer. The friars struck at the intruders with their lighted candles and crucifixes, putting them to sudden flight, for they believed themselves attacked by a company of angels.

In spite of Savonarola's entreaties, new encounters with the assailants followed, the convent bell was tolled, and every moment the tumult heightened. The convent seemed to be gaining the victory when a new proclamation was received from the Signoria, stating that all who did not leave the convent within an hour would be considered rebels. And now the tide of war changed and the assailants were triumphant, and Giovacchino della Vecchia, who commanded the palace guard, threatened to destroy the convent buildings with his artillery if Savonarola, Fra Domenico, and Fra Salvestro were not given up. Savonarola's friends entreated him to escape, by being let down the wall on a side that had not been reached by his adversaries: but Savonarola chose to surrender; so did his faithful friend, Fra Domenico. Fra Salvestro concealed himself, and was not found until the next day.

Villari thus describes the scene: "The two friends had no sooner come down into the cloisters than the mob, pressing around them, gave a shout of ferocious joy. All were now insane with rage. It was eight o'clock in the evening. The dense mob looked like a tumultuous sea of helmets, cuirasses, swords, and spears, from which the light of lanterns

and torches was dimly reflected. The people gazed
on Savonarola with threatening looks, and holding
up their lanterns to his face, exclaimed: 'This is
the true light!' They scorched and burned his face
with their flambeaux, saying, 'Now for a turn of the
key!' They twisted his fingers, and beat him; in-
sultingly calling out: 'Prophesy now to us who it
was that beat you!' So great was their fury, that
the guards could with difficulty protect him, by
crossing their arms and shields over him."

When they reached the palace, the two friars
were brought before the Gonfaloniere to be interrogated. He asked if they asserted that their words
came from God, and when they replied in the afir-
mative, caused them to be thrown into separate cells.
On the morrow, Fra Salvestro was seized and incar-
cerated.

On the 11th of April, the Signoria appointed a
committee of seventeen examiners to conduct the
trial of the three monks, and gave permission for
the use of torture. Among this committee were the
deadliest, most open enemies of Savonarola — Piero
degli Alberti, who exhibited fierce hatred on the day
of the ordeal; and Dolfo Spini, the ferocious leader
of the Compagnacci, who headed the tumult on Ascension Day, and also when the convent was attacked
—who had tried to kill Savonarola by means of

hired assassins — who had even made the attempt with his own hands, and been frustrated by Savonarola's guard of friends.

Savonarola was questioned, and, remaining firm in his replies, the unhappy friar, in spite of his delicate and debilitated frame, his sensitive nature and nervous temperament, was at once subjected to the torture of the hoisting rope. In this kind of torture a rope is attached to a pulley on a high pole, the victim has his hands tied behind his back, and the end of the rope wound around his wrists. He is then repeatedly drawn up and let down suddenly by the executioner; the arms, drawn up backward, are made to describe a semicircle; the pain of the torn muscles and fibres is excruciating. The agony often produces delirium, and, if protracted, death.

That Savonarola had a shuddering fear of physical pain, that he was unable to support its effects, it would be impossible to deny. He had high mental courage, but his *physique* lacked all power of resistance, and was keenly susceptible to outward impressions. As soon as he was subjected to the torture, his mind began to wander, his answers were incoherent, and he wailed out, in his paroxysms of agony, "O Lord! take, oh, take my life!" The executioner stated that he had never seen any one on whom the torture produced so immediate and so severe an effect.

During a month he was repeatedly tortured, and the historians Pico and Burlamacchi testify that when he was drawn up by the rope, live coals were applied to the soles of his feet.

There seems to have been no doubt in the minds of the historians of that day, that the minutes of his examination, during torture, were grossly falsified; they are in many instances contradictory, and sometimes unintelligible. They represent Savonarola denying, in his agony, that he spoke from Divine inspiration, or had visions, or prophesied, and then reasserting that these things were true.

He was much lowered in the estimation of his few remaining disciples by his incapacity to endure the torture, and remain coherent and firm in his declarations.

But in spite of all his delirious ravings, and in spite of the transparent falsification of the minutes, the Signoria found, to their dismay, that Savonarola could not be proved guilty of any charge brought against him. They had succeeded in humiliating him, and wholly destroying the faith reposed in him by his followers. This was their only triumph; yet it was one of importance, for it rendered his condemnation easier.

Savonarola was compelled, before eight witnesses, to sign the copy of his own depositions, but Burlamacchi asserts that one copy was read to him, and then a different one dexterously substituted for his signature.

During his respite from torture, Villari says, "His troubled and wearied mind soon took the direction of mystical contemplations. His prison became peopled by supernatural creations, by invisible beings, and when once carried off to that world, every other thought vanished from his mind." In these moments he forgot all the horrors he had undergone; forgot his lacerated limbs, his insatiable persecutors, his prison walls, and imagined himself in the pulpit of the Duomo. His pen was not idle, and he wrote his last meditations or sermons, taking for his text the Psalmist's words, "In thee, O Lord, do I put my trust; let me never be confounded."

Pope Borgia sent on two commissioners to examine Savonarola under fresh torture. On the 20th of May he was cruelly interrogated before them. On the 21st the torture was repeated, and he was ordered to appear upon the 23d, to hear his sentence. As the minutes of this examination more clearly proved the innocence of Savonarola than the previous ones had done, they were not signed, nor printed, nor publicly read, according to the established custom. Sentence of death was hastily passed upon the three friars, without a single accusation against them having been proved. Savonarola begged to be allowed to see his condemned brethren. The friars met for the first time, after forty days of imprisonment and torture.

The undaunted and immovable Fra Domenico had borne the most severe tortures without flinching, never betraying his sufferings, and never wavering in his assertions. Fra Salvestro, who was a natural somnambulist, and whose organization was, if possible, even more sensitive than that of Savonarola, had yielded at once to his persecutors, and to escape the agony he could not endure, had admitted or denied whatever was required of him.

After the interview, Savonarola, on returning to his cell, quickly fell asleep. It is related that during his sleep he seemed to dream, that he smiled, and his countenance expressed the most perfect serenity.

The next morning he administered the sacrament to the two friars, and took the communion himself. At the close of the ceremony, it was announced to the condemned that they were to be conducted to the Piazza della Signoria — that Piazza where the little children, taught by Savonarola, had substi-

tuted hymns for licentious carnival songs; had solicited alms for the poor, instead of waylaying the
passer by, and emptying his purse to spend its contents in feasting and carousing; that Piazza where
Savonarola had built for them the pyramid upon
which their earnest young hands had laid the vanities they had collected from the penitent, and made
them into a bonfire.

Three tribunals had been erected on the *ringhi-
era*. The first, next to the door of the palace, was
appropriated to the Bishop of Vasova; the second
to the Pope's Commissioners; the third was occupied by the Gonfaloniere (Mayor) and the Otto
(Eight Rulers). In front was a scaffold supporting
an upright beam, holding another beam, near the
top, at right angles. An arm of this beam had
been truncated, to diminish its resemblance to a
cross. From the beam were suspended three halters and three chains. At its foot lay a large heap
of combustible materials. The friars were sentenced to be hanged from the halters; the chains were
then to be wound around their bodies, which were
to be suspended until consumed.

The three friars, when they had descended the
stairs of the palace, were ordered to lay aside their
gowns. Their scanty woollen under-tunics alone remained; their feet were bare. Savonarola showed

great emotion when he received this insulting command; but resistance would have been fruitless; and he obeyed, saying: "Holy dress, how much I longed to wear thee! Thou wast granted to me by the grace of God, and to this day I have kept thee spotless. I do not now leave thee; thou art taken from me!"

Their hands were then tied, and they were led out into the Piazza, up to the first tribunal, where the Bishop of Vasova was seated. The Bishop was compelled to obey the orders of the Pope; but he appeared to be greatly agitated, for he loved Savonarola, and had been one of his disciples. He pronounced the funeral ceremony with a feeble and broken voice. The gowns of the friars were restored to them, that they might be first degraded, and then have their sacred vestments removed for the last time. It is said that the Bishop's presence of mind so completely forsook him, that he forgot the words of the formula, and taking hold of Savonarola's arm, exclaimed: "I separate thee from the Church Militant and Triumphant!" Savonarola electrified the bystanders by solemnly replying, "Militant, — *yours* is not Triumphant!"

The gowns of the friars having been stripped off in token of their degradation, they were led up to the Pope's Commissioners, from whom they heard

their sentence as heretics. Then they were placed
before the Otto, who, according to the established
custom, put the sentence to vote, and passed it without an opposing voice. The condemned were then
conducted to the scaffold. Savonarola's composure
was never once disturbed, and his companions were
equally calm. The ferocious mob hooted and jeered
at them, and gave utterance to all manner of con-
tumely, but the martyrs continued as serene as
though the revilings were unheard. Savonarola's
last words were, " The Lord has suffered as much
for me ! " The two friars were executed first. The
halter suspended from the centre of the beam was
left for Savonarola. When he mounted the scaffold, after witnessing the death of his companions
in persecution, he saw the people, with lighted torches, crowding eagerly to the beam, impatient to light
the fire, before the spirit had escaped. A voice
from the crowd cried out, " Prophet, now is the time
to perform a miracle ! "

The executioner, to please the brutal mob, in-
dulged in audible jokes. While the body of Savonarola was yet alive and quivering, he made great
haste, hoping that the fire would reach the martyr
before life was extinct, but owing to this very speed
the chain, which he was trying to wind around the
body, slipped from his hand, and, during the brief

delay occasioned by his efforts to recover it, Savonarola passed into the Eternal World.

He died in the forty-fifth year of his age. This martyrdom took place at ten o'clock in the morning, on the 23d of May, 1498.

At first a current of wind turned away the flames from the three bodies; then the fickle populace, easily swayed by the most trifling incident, cried, out, "A miracle! A miracle!" But the wind soon fell, and the flames rose and enveloped the bodies.

Still the morbidly excited imaginations of the people made them eager to discover some miraculous token; and when the flames caught the cords by which the hands of Savonarola were pinioned, and the heat caused the hand to move, they declared that he had raised his right arm in the midst of the flames to bless his enemies, who were burning him! His disciples fell upon their knees, sobbing wildly, and men and women lamented aloud.

The Arrabbiati could not endure this sight; they hired little children to make a noise, and dance, and throw stones at the burning bodies. The favorite, barbarous game of stone-throwing, which Savonarola had partially abolished, was thus re-established in the presence of his corpse, and was entered into with so much zest, that large pieces of flesh were cut from their bodies by the sharp stones, and fell, hissing, into the flames beneath.

Many ladies, disguised as servants, made their way through the crowd to the scaffold, to gather up relics ; but the soldiers of the Signoria drove them back. The Signoria, fearing that the very ashes of the martyrs might be made to work some miracle, had them collected and thrown over the Ponte Vecchio into the Arno.

But even there those ashes did not prove inaccessible. Villari tells us that young "Pico della Mirandola although an eminent scholar and learned in philosophy, believed that he had been able to pick up from the Arno a part of Savonarola's heart, and he asserted that he again and again had had experience of its miraculous effects in curing many diseases, and exorcising malignant spirits."

Henceforward the friars of the Convent of St. Mark were relentlessly persecuted by the Arrabbiati, who were now masters of the city; they were robbed, under various pretexts, and deprived of their privileges and freedom. To show to what an absurd extent the Arrabbiati carried their animosity, we cannot forbear mentioning, that, after much deliberation, they declared the great bell of the convent, which went by the name of Piagnona, guilty of having tolled on the day of the tumult, and they accordingly banished it from Florence. It was taken down and carried without the city, in a cart, and publicly whipped by the hangman, with as much gravity as though all who witnessed the punishment actually believed that it was endowed with sensation.

Only a few years later, when the Spanish army had replaced the Medici in power over Florence; when all Italy was scourged; when Clement VII. became Pope, and Charles V. sacked the Eternal City; when churches were converted into barracks for soldiers and stables for horses — the prophecies of Savonarola seemed fulfilled to the letter. Men never tired of pointing out how the events he had foretold literally came to pass: his sermons were in every one's hand, and the Convent of St. Mark became the powerful centre of the most faithful friends of liberty and lovers of their native land.

Well might Mrs. Browning say of Savonarola:

> "'Tis true that when the dust of death has choked
> A great man's voice, the common words he said
> Turn oracles."

VITTORIA COLONNA.

Who ever walked through the Colonna Gallery at Rome without pausing before the portrait of Vittoria Colonna, the great Italian poetess? The face is one of surpassing beauty — singularly pure in outline and perfect in regularity of feature ; the eyes are large, soft, contemplative ; the forehead grand ; the lips full and finely curved; the hair of that molten gold which haunted Titian's dreams, and became tresses of sunshine upon his canvas. Rarely has an angelic spirit, affluent in intellectual gifts, been enshrined in mortal mould of such absolute loveliness; for Vittoria Colonna's "clayey part" was but a faint reflex of the gloriously beautiful shape within.

In olden days, as in modern, poetesses seldom looked poetical; true hearts and noble minds were often disguised in earthly cerements of coarse and unshapely clay. That "*something in this world amiss*," which, Tennyson tells us, "shall be unriddled by and by," creates a want of harmony between the inner and the outer development.   Well may we contemplate with refreshing delight such an exception to this perplexing rule of incongruity as the Italian poetess presents.

Vittoria Colonna was the daughter of Fabrizio Colonna, brother of that prothonotary Colonna, who was decapitated, after tortures of inconceivable cruelty, at the instigation of the hereditary enemies of his family, the Orsini, and by the order of Pope Sixtus IV. Vittoria's mother was Agnes of Montefelre, daughter of Frederick, Duke of Urbino.

At the time of Vittoria's birth (1490), the princely house of Colonna had reached its meridian splendor. Vittoria was born at Marino. The castle and town picturesquely nestle among the hills that surround the lovely lake of Albano, and of the many fiefs held by the Colonna in the neighborhood of Rome, this was considered the most beautiful.

When the Colonna took service under Frederick II. of Naples, that king, to render more secure his hold over his new and powerful friends, betrothed the infant Vittoria, then five years of age, to Ferdinand d'Avalos, a child of the same age, son of Alphonso, Marquis of Pescara.

Costanza d'Avalos, Duchess of Francavilla, the

elder sister of the boy *fiancée*, was one of the most cultivated, pure, and highly refined women of her day. Shortly after the betrothal of the children, the Marquis of Pescara lost his life, through the treachery of a black slave. The young Ferdinand was his heir, and, on the death of Costanza's husband, King Ferdinand made her *châtelaine* of the picturesque little island of Ischia. The infant Vittoria was then transferred to her charge, to receive her education in company with her future bridegroom.

A year later, King Ferdinand II. died, deeply lamented by every class of his people, and especially mourned at Ischia.

When the children were eleven years old, the harmonious routine of their days of blended study and pastime was broken by the presence of discrowned royalty. The French had sacked Capua, and were advancing upon Naples; and Frederick, the last of the Aragonese kings, with his queen and children, sought refuge on the rock-bound island of Ischia until he threw himself upon the generosity of the French king.

Love seems to have been equally strong in the hearts of both affianced children. When the youthful couple had entered their nineteenth year, Costanza deemed it time for their marriage to be celebrated.　Vittoria made a farewell visit to her parents at Marino, and returned to Ischia, escorted by a large company of Roman nobles, who came to be present at her nuptials.

In beauty of person the young Pescara seems to have been a fitting mate for Vittoria.　His biographer, Giani, thus describes him : " His beard was auburn, his nose aquiline, his eyes large and fiery when excited, but mild and gentle at other times."

He had many knightly accomplishments, but his bearing was haughty, his speech brief and grave, and he kept aloof from all familiar intercourse; to Vittoria, however, he was all gentleness and tenderness.

After their nuptials, two years of tranquil and uninterrupted joy, such as mortals seldom taste, were granted the youthful pair.　Later in life, Vittoria often and often recurs to her blessed childhood, and to those two years of unbroken, ecstatic felicity, in her happy island home.

But Pescara was a soldier; not to fight as soon as he reached manhood, was to be dishonored.　At the close of those two idyllic years, when he was, twenty-one, he accompanied Vittoria's father, and joined the army in Lombardy.

Severely as the young husband and wife suffered from this separation, even the gentle, clinging Vittoria never sought to be spared the pang of parting; she never forgot that she was the daughter and the wife of a soldier. When it was suggested that her husband was the sole surviving scion of a noble house, and ought to be absolved from risking his life upon the battle-field, she repelled the counsel as indignantly as the young soldier himself. Courageously she sent him forth with the olden motto on his shield, " *With* this, or *on* this."

Vittoria remained at Ischia with Costanza. The dwellers on the little island were always surrounded by a brilliant circle of wits, and poets, and literary men, whose society both ladies thoroughly enjoyed. There was no fear of scandal, for even the foulest tongue would not have dared to sully Vittoria's name by the suggestion that she was consoled for the absence of her husband by the admiration of other men.

In his very first battle, Pescara was made prisoner. Vittoria's father met the same fate. The united Spanish and Papal arms were defeated by the French, before Ravenna, 9th of April, 1512. Pescara was picked up on the field, where he had been left for dead, and carried captive to Milan. During his imprisonment he composed a "Dialogo d'Amore," which he inscribed and sent to his wife.

3*

The Bishop of Como asserts that this dialogue was full of grave and witty thoughts.

Pangs of sorrow gave birth to Vittoria's muse. The first poetic production was a letter, in verse, of one hundred and twelve lines, addressed to her husband in his prison. One naturally smiles at the *pun* which breaks in upon her lamentations, but when we remember the elegantly turned puns of Shakespeare's heroines, involuntarily uttered in the most agonizing situations, we must pardon the Italian poetess for saying, —

"Se Vittoria volevi, io t'era appresso,
Ma tu, lasciandome, lasciavi lei. "

"If *victory* was thy desire, *I* was by thy side; but in leaving *me*, thou didst leave also *her*."

Pescara's captivity was robbed of much of its discomfort through the influence of a general in the service of France, who had married the prisoner's aunt. As soon as his wounds were healed, he was permitted to ransom himself for six thousand ducats. Vittoria had the great joy of welcoming her husband once more to their island home.

The maternal principle was strongly developed in her affectionate nature, and the holy presence of infancy soon became indispensable to her perfect felicity — but she remained childless.

Her husband had a young cousin, Alfonso d'Avalos, Marchese del Vasto, whose disposition was so violent and ungovernable, that guardians, tutors, servants, alike shrank from him in terror. Every attempt to train or educate him had proved futile; yet he was endowed with fine mental capacities, and with personal beauty of the highest order. This boy Vittoria fearlessly adopted, declaring that he only needed prudent and loving management to become a superior man. The boy was quickly inspired with a sort of chivalric devotion for her; his passionate nature, rightly moulded and directed, proved to be full of strength and nobility. She magnetized to the surface every dormant good impulse, and cultivated his heart as well as his mind. He owed to her his love of literature and his scholarly attainments. The turbulent youth became a refined, whole-souled man, and a soldier of renown. Vittoria had ample cause to rejoice over the fruition of her glorious work, and Alfonso's ever-enduring love brightened her life in its darkest hours. She used to say, with exultation, that the reproach of being childless should be removed from her name, for she had given mental birth to a child in developing the mind and moral nature of a being whom no other hand had been able to master.

After a few months of domestic happiness, Pescara joined the army in Lombardy.

Vittoria remained at Ischia, surrounded, as before, by poets and men of letters. Some of the most celebrated writers in Europe visited her little island, and immortalized its beauties. Tasso was among their number; he eloquently celebrates the brilliant Ischia reunions of choice spirits. Vittoria had herself become an enthusiastic votary of the muse, and her lyre was never more silent.

Pescara's duties in camp only permitted him at long intervals to pay brief visits to Ischia. In October, 1522, he remained with Vittoria three days, and then returned to the army. Battle quickly succeeded battle, and she never saw him more.

At the age of thirty-five, he was made general-in-chief to Charles V., but, in spite of his undeniable valor and soldierly achievements, the proofs that he was false to his king are only too strong.

Pope Clement VII. tempted him to turn traitor to Charles, and use the armies under his command to crush the Spanish power in Italy. The throne of Naples was promised him as the price of his treason. Pescara undoubtedly entertained the overtures, but it chanced that a messenger, bearing letters which would have revealed the whole conspiracy, was robbed and murdered, by an innkeeper at Bergamo, and buried under a staircase. As time passed and no tidings were received, the conspirators concluded that the letters had been forcibly taken from their courier, and the blot would be made known to Charles. Pescara determined to save his own reputation by a clever stratagem. He wrote to Charles, and coupled with assurances of the greatest loyalty the information that certain conspirators had made him propositions to which he had listened for the sake of detecting and frustrating their machinations.

This complicity is too strongly proved by a letter from Vittoria, in which she vehemently urges her husband not to be lured from the path of honor by any temptations, and tells him that she has " no wish to be the wife of *a king,* but only of a *loyal and upright man.*"

It is thought by some historians that this letter, and not the disappearance of the messenger, saved Pescara from becoming a traitor to his monarch.

Charles credited Pescara's tale, and made him generalissimo of the imperial forces in Italy. In the same year he was taken ill, at Milan, and sent for Vittoria. She set out with all speed, but had only reached Viterbo when she received the tidings of his death. He died on the 25th of November, 1525, was buried at Milan, but shortly afterward carried to Naples, and interred with great pomp.

Vittoria's love had been boundless, and her sorrow

had no limit. She gave herself up to the most frantic bewailing, "not comforted to live," because Pescara was gone.

And what manner of man wâs it who inspired love
so large and grief so great? Some paragon of virtue,
doubtless! Alas! for the truth. The reader starts
in amazement and shrinks in horror at learning what
all history testifies. This idol, raised for heart-wor-
ship by one of the purest, loveliest, most gifted of
God's creatures, was a man base and infamous, cruel
as a savage, merciless as a heathen. Two virtues he
had, and apparently *only two* — he was a brave soldier, and he loved Vittoria.

"He was reckless of human suffering," says the
historian, "and eminent even among his fellow-cap-
tains for the ferocity and often wantonness of the
ravages and wide-spread misery he wrought." "The
cruelty he committed was worse than Turks would
have been guilty of."

An anecdote illustrates his pitiless sternness as a
disciplinarian. He had ordered the ears of a soldier
to be cut off for entering a house for the purpose of
plunder. The man implored that his ears might be
spared, and he cried out in his anguish that death
would be preferable to losing them. Pescara, with
savage jocoseness, at once bade his soldiers, since the
culprit *preferred* death, to hang him to a neighbor-

ing tree. In vain the wretch shrieked for mercy —
he was seized and hanged, while Pescara enjoyed
the joke of having taken him at his word.

Guicciardini states that he has often heard the
Chancellor Morone declare "that there did not exist
a worse or more faithless man in all Italy than Pescara."

And this is the man whom Vittoria's love sur-
rounds with such a radiant halo, that his character
seems resplendent with the most glorious virtues;
this is the man whom she makes the theme of a long
series of poems "in memoriam"—the man whom
she calls her *bel sole*, for whose dear sake she is tor-
mented to commit suicide, whom she longs for
death to rejoin, and then chides herself for wishing
to die, because haply *her virtue may not suffice to
enable her to rejoin him* in the mansions of the
blest! Can love's power to *idealize* be more forcibly and wondrously illustrated?

She had entered her thirty-sixth year when she
became a widow, and the writers of that day pronounce her beauty in its meridian glory. The medals struck at Milan, just before her husband's death,
bear witness to her supreme loveliness. She was,
even then, styled the most celebrated woman in
Italy, but her renown as a poetess became much
greater at a later period.

The first stunning prostration of her grief caused Vittoria to attempt to shut herself out wholly and forever from that world which she had hitherto found so beautiful and so full of enjoyment. She hastened to Rome, and immured herself in the convent of San Silvestro, resolved to take the veil. But the Bishop of Carpentras, a man of letters and a poet, Vittoria's personal friend, saw the fatal rashness of the act into which grief had hurried her, and induced Pope Clement to send a letter to the abbess and nuns of San Silvestro, charging them to shelter and console the Marchesa di Pescara, but absolutely forbidding them to let her take the veil.

She had resided at the convent nearly a year when a new quarrel arose between the Colonna family and the Pope. Vittoria's brother, Ascanio, her sole protector, now insisted upon her leaving the convent and hastening to Marino. A little later the Colonna faction sacked the Vatican and the houses of their mortal enemies, the Orsini. For this act of violence, Cardinal Colonna was deprived of his hat, and the estates of all the family were confiscated.

Vittoria once more took up her abode in the little island which had borne the footprints of her husband's feet, from infancy to manhood — which had been the scene of such rich joys, and was now the grave of so many hopes. Her first passionate burst of anguish had softened into a quiet mournfulness, and from that time her true poetical career may be said to have begun. Writing poetry became the chief occupation of her life. One hundred and thirty-four of her sonnets were lamentations over her loss, or written in honor of her husband's memory. The distinguished men and women of that day hailed with delight the appearance of each new poetical effusion, and wrote in its praise to the sorrowing songstress. Her works passed into three editions during her lifetime — which in that day was equivalent to thirty in this.

It is a remarkable fact, that this beautiful and gifted woman, who had all her life been the centre of a crowd of worshippers, so thoroughly impressed every one who knew her with the sense of her perfect purity, that she seems to have been the rare exception to the rule which prevents the chastest from escaping calumny.

Numerous suitors she, of course, had, but when she refused the hand which had been once bestowed with her heart, and could never be given again, ardent lovers became devoted and life-long friends.

Trollope says; " We find her uninfluenced by the bitter hereditary hatreds of her family, striving to act as peace-maker between hostile factions, and weeping over the mischief occasioned by their struggles. We find her the constant correspondent and valued friend of almost every good and great man of her day." He adds: "The learned and elegant Bembo writes of her, that he considered her poetical judgment as sound and authoritative as that of the greatest masters of the art of song." Guidiccioni, the poetical Bishop of Fossombrone, and one of Paul III.'s ablest diplomats, declares that the ancient glory of Tuscany had altogether passed into Latium in her person; and sends her sonnets of his own, with earnest entreaties that she will point out the faults. Veronica Gambara, herself a poetess, of merit perhaps not inferior to that of Vittoria, professed herself her most ardent admirer, and engaged Rinaldo Corso to write the commentary on her poems, which he executed as we have seen. Bernardo Tasso made her the subject of several of his poems. Giovii dedicated to her his life of Pescara, and Cardinal Pompeo Colonna his book "On the Praises of Women," and Contarini paid her the far more remarkable compliment of dedicating to her his work on "Free Will."

In 1530, the pestilence raged in Naples, and even reached Ischia. Vittoria was compelled to fly to Rome. The Colonna family had made their peace with Pope Clement, and their fiefs had been restored to them. The Poetess resided with her brother Ascanio and his beautiful and accomplished wife, Donna Giovanna d'Aragona. Vittoria's adopted son and pupil, the Marchese del Vasto, was also at Rome, and his presence was always a joy to her. Yet she grew restless and ill at ease away from her island home, and hastened back, as soon as safety permitted.

At the close of six years, she was again induced by her brother and adopted son to visit Rome. Her fame had increased with every year, and it is recorded that her stay in Rome was one continued ovation.

Her religious impulses were strong and pure, and she was prompted to the study of theology that she might know something of the God whom she worshipped. A year after this visit to the holy city she first evinced Protestant tendencies. Renée of France had married Hercules II., whose sympathies were avowedly with the Protestant party. These sympathies had rendered the Court of Ferrara the resort, and in some instances the refuge, of many professors of the new ideas which were beginning to agitate Italy. Vittoria visited Ferrara for the purpose of exchanging views upon this vexed question with some of the leading minds assembled there.

Duke Hercules and his court paid her the highest

honors, and invited the most distinguished poets and men of letters in Venice and Lombardy to meet her.

At Ferrara, she conceived the idea of making a journey to the Holy Land, though she was then in failing health. Her adopted son went to Ferrara to dissuade her, and after much entreaty, induced her to return to Rome instead. Her presence in the Papal capital was once more the signal for public rejoicings.

That she was an advocate of religious reform, her poetry gives ample testimony, though her Italian biographers make great efforts to maintain her orthodoxy. Trollope declares that " Vittoria Colonna has survived in men's minds as a poetess. But she is far more interesting to the historical student who would obtain a full understanding of that wonderful sixteenth century, as a *Protestant.* Her highly gifted and richly cultivated intelligence, her great social position, and above all her close intimacy with the eminent men who strove to set on foot an Italian reformation which should not be incompatible with the Papacy, made the illustration of her religious opinions a matter of no slight historical interest."

It was shortly after her return to Rome from Ferrara, in the year 1537, that a tender and durable friendship sprang up between the renowned poetess and the great sculptor and painter, Michael Angelo. He was in his sixty-third year, and she in her forty-seventh. It was through his association with Vittoria Colonna, that the rugged, stern, self-intelligent old man became a devout Christian. In the poems which he addresses to her, he attributes that change wholly to her influence.

The letters of Vittoria to Michael Angelo are preserved as the most treasured possessions of his descendants. The last was written after the sculptor became architect of St. Peters, and she tells him playfully that her duties to the youthful inmates of the Convent of St. Catherine, at Viterbo, and his duties as architect at St. Peter's, must prevent a frequent correspondence.

In this same year, 1544, she returned from Viterbo to Rome, and took up her residence in the Convent of the Benedictines of St. Anne. Her health, long delicate, now began to fail rapidly. When she became seriously worse, she was removed from the convent to the house (which chanced to be near) of the only one of her kindred then left in Rome — Giuliano Cesarini, the husband of Giulia Colonna.

Her brother and son were both at a distance, but Michael Angelo, her ever true and devotedly attached friend, sat beside her couch as her pure and lovely spirit gained its freedom.   It is said that he often mourned in remembering that he had not dared to press his lips for the only time, upon the noble but clay-cold forehead.

She died in February, 1554, in the fifty-seventh year of her age.

Vittoria well knew that her works were a more lasting monument than could be carved out of stone, and she ordered that her funeral should closely resemble that given to the nuns in the convent where she had resided ; and like theirs her place of sepulture remains unmarked.

GALILEO'S VILLA.

CHIEF among the memorable villas which girdle Florence, and have been consecrated by the foot-prints of the illustrious dead, are the villas in which the renowned Galileo resided — the villa where he lived and hoped and rejoiced! the villa where he suffered, despaired, and died!

The villa *del Gioiello*, usually called Galileo's villa, is situated beyond the hill Arcetri. It is an ivy-draped, gloomy, desolate-looking abode, and the heavy atmosphere of the place is rendered more oppressive by the melancholy inscription on the outer wall, which records that in this villa the great astronomer and philosopher passed the closing years of his life, afflicted with blindness, the victim of Papal persecution, abandoned by his powerful Medicean patrons; but still surrounded by a few faithful friends, who reverently received the last inspirations of his towering genius.

Not far from this villa is the rude tower called Galileo's observatory.

But it is in the quaint old villa which crowns the lovely height of *Bellosquardo*, and is also celebrated as the residence of *Guicardini*, the historian, Galileo's contemporary and friend, that Galileo passed fourteen years before bigotry's iron heel crushed out of his heart every buoyant and expectant throb, and before the hand of affliction had drawn the pall of blindness between him and that glorious firmament whose luminaries, watched by his speculative eyes, had filled the world with the new light of science.

There is a bust of Galileo near the northern entrance of the villa, with a tablet chronicling his residence within those walls.

Upon what is now called the *Piazza di Bello-squardo*, opens the somewhat imposing gateway which leads to the front entrance of the villa, through a brief carriage-path, lined on either side with laurustinus, arbutus, yellow jessamine, cluster roses, with a few fine trees shooting far above the flowering shrubbery. The grounds are by no means extensive, but they are so dexterously laid out in winding walks, dotted by tiny gardens, with here and there sudden openings among the trees, disclosing the most enchanting views, that they produce the effect of both space and variety.

It is said that Galileo had a passion for flowers,

and delighted in cultivating his garden with his own hands. What aspect these limited pleasure-grounds must have presented nearly two centuries and a half ago, it is not difficult to conjecture; for Galileo, who trod them for fourteen years, could not have cherished his floral tastes in such a suggestive locality, without causing that teeming earth to bloom out into even fuller, richer beauty than it boasts at the present day.

This villa was formerly called villa *Albizzi*, but it now bears the name of *Villa dell' Ombrellino* — Villa of the Little Umbrella. It received this designation from a rudely shaped species of wooden umbrella, with a circular bench running round the stem. This unpoetical-looking substitute for a summer-house stands in the northwest corner of the grounds, which juts out over a green valley, and overlooks a charming prospect. The Italians have so decided a passion for nicknames, that after this extraordinary umbrella bower once made its appearance, they, doubtless, could not be induced to call the villa by any high-sounding title. The little umbrella can be seen far down the road towards Florence before the villa itself is visible — it is consequently the *Villa dell' Ombrellino* to every Italian. And a most delightful retreat the unpicturesque *Umbrella* affords. To one perched upon the circular seat, in days we could tell of, it was a never-failing enjoyment to watch the changing aspect of the surrounding scenery ; for with every alternation of light the landscape varies, some new charm is evoked by the play of the sunshine, and some loveliness, very palpable before, has disappeared in the shadow.

But the prospect revealed from this clumsy, yet cosy resting-place is far surpassed by that which the terrace commands. The centre of the roof of the villa, a square of about twenty feet, is flat, and surrounded by an iron railing. Furnished with sofas, table, and chairs, it makes a most fascinating terrace drawing-room. There before you lies the whole city of Florence, with its stately palaces, and ancient churches, and striking towers, standing out clearly against the blue sky, or only dimly suggested by shadowy, dreamy outlines, through the golden-grey mist · of morning or evening; and there is the vine and olive clad valley of the Arno; and there is the *Cascine*, the favorite promenade or drive, the Hyde Park of Florence ; and there is the *Poggio Imperiale*, and, leading to it, that

> "———— abrupt, black line of cypresses
> Which sign the way to Florence ;"

and *Fiesole*, the ever beautiful; and *San Miniato*, with *Michel Angelo's* fortifications; and the en-

MICHAEL ANGELO'S FORTIFICATION, SAN MINIATO.

circling Appennines; the hills of Vallombrosa and Carrara; and on every side countless villas gemming the landscape, and teeming with romantic histories; and all down the undulating slopes of the *Bellosquardo* hill, the greenly fertile farms displaying their treasures of grapes and olives and figs.

But who could venture to describe the glorious and ever-varying sunsets watched from that terrace, or the marvels conjured to heighten the landscape when the molten moonlight lent its own mysterious beauty to the scene? But when the moon was absent, and even when the stars were obscured, Florence was still visible, outlined by her myriad lights; and on the evenings of her illuminations, those outlines were clothed with a flickering garment of fire, wonderful to behold.

In 1863 and 1864, the writer was a member of the little circle that occupied this villa, and that terrace, where Galileo once gazed upon the stars, was the favorite place of gathering in the summer evenings. Here tea was served, and guests were received. Often from this terrace the melodious voice of the songstress has floated over the hills, and enraptured the ears of listeners in the neighboring villas. And, strange to relate, this terrace now and then witnessed rehearsals of the little dramas, afterwards performed at the English Dramatic Drawing Room, by the company of amateurs who in the winter of 1864 and 1865 devoted their talents to charities.

Once, during our sojourn in the Galileo villa, its spacious old entrance hall was the scene of a dramatic representation, peculiarly appropriate to a Florentine locality. The play was entitled " The Unknown Masterpiece" (a free translation of the *Chef d'œuvre de l'Inconnu*). The great Florentine sculptor and painter, Michel Angelo, was one of the heroes (personated by an American sculptor of talent). The Grand Duke of Florence, Casino de' Medici, was represented by a descendant of the *Buonnaroti* family, from which Michel Angelo sprang. The heroine was embodied by a lovely golden-haired American maiden, whose delicious voice has given her a foremost rank among the nightingales of Florence. A youthful page was played by the marvellously gifted little daughter of T. A. Trollope, who enchanted the audience by her wonderful vocalization. The young girl, who afterwards evinced so much talent at the Dramatic Drawing Room, made her *début* on the occasion, as the bewitching boy-student, brother of the young sculptor who was the hero of the drama. The latter character was admirably personated by a rising young artist, also a leading member of the Dramatic Drawing Room company.

Such a festival seemed particularly appropriate within walls which the presence of Galileo had consecrated, for he was himself a great lover of the drama, and declaimed with much effect. He delighted in music, and performed with so much skill upon several instruments, especially the lute, that he had been counselled in his youth to become a professional musician.

In truth, Galileo was rich in accomplishments, for he was also a proficient in drawing, and evinced a taste for all the arts; besides possessing very wide information, a fondness for literature, and great command of his pen.

Galileo Galilei was born at Pisa in 1564. His family was noble. His father designed him for a physician. He entered the University of Pisa at an early age, and quickly distinguished himself. He had not completed his twenty-fifth year when he filled the chair of Professor of Mathematics.

In the cathedral of Pisa the stranger is still pointed out the lamp which suggested to Galileo, by its slow and uniform swinging, the possibility of a pendulum as the motive power of clocks. He was then only eighteen years of age. He wrote some remarkable essays based upon the motion of this lamp, but it was not until nearly half a century later that he actually succeeded in making a pendulum clock.

It seems almost incredible, that the man who invented the thermometer, improved the compass, constructed the telescope, which disclosed to him the irregular surface of the moon, caused by her valleys and mountains ; the spots upon the sun, and showed that the Milky Way, was a lengthened cluster of countless stars — that the man who revealed to the world these unimagined facts, and who confirmed and promulgated the truth already made known by Copernicus, that the planets revolved about the sun, which is the centre of our system — that this man should have been all his life surrounded by enemies and detractors, should have lived through a series of relentless persecutions, to die their victim. A frank but incautious criticism sowed the rapid-springing seed of Galileo's first disgrace.

Giovanni de Medici, natural son of Casimo I., had invented a machine, which he submitted to the young Galileo. Giovanni was a poor engineer, and a worse architect, as the tomb of St. Lawrence, for which he furnished the design, testifies. Galileo, who had not yet learned the humiliating lesson, that policy is expediency, when princes and potentates are to be dealt with, publicly criticised the invention. Sentence of banishment was the result of this te-

merity. He took refuge in Venice, and remained
in exile for eighteen years. He rapidly achieved
celebrity. Very soon he was elected professor of
mathematics at Padua. There he published a treatise on fortifications, one on mechanics, and an admirable work on proportions.

But Galileo yearned for Florence ; and his biographers relate, with somewhat severe comments, that
he availed himself of an occasion to be restored to
the good graces of the *Medici*, by a delicate piece
of flattery. One of his most important telescopic
revelations was the discovery of the satellites of
Jupiter. He gave them the name of *satellites of
the Medici*, and published in Padua his treatise on
these satellites. This compliment threw open the
closed gates of his country; he received permission
to return to Florence, and joyfully availed himself
of the longed-for privilege.

His honest ingenuousness had banished him — a
stroke of policy effected his recall. He bowed to
the exigencies of the times. It was his nature to
conciliate, rather than to combat, his opponents.
All through his life, either from timidity or from
an instinctive shrinking from strife, he tried to avoid
contest. He strove to win, to convince, to influence
— not to oppose. Thus we too often find him ap-

4*

parently yielding to those who are too obviously in
the wrong, instead of combating their errors.

In that age, any deviation from accepted dogmas
was called heresy; and nothing ruined a man more
quickly and more certainly than the accusation of
heresy.

Galileo was at heart a sincere Catholic. He loved
and had perfect faith in the doctrines of the Church,
and he believed in the Scriptures. When the clergy
declared to him that the discoveries he had made, if
veritable, contradicted revealed religion, and were
wholly at variance with Scriptural statements, it did
not shake his faith in the religion of revelation. He
knew that the facts which he had proclaimed were
unquestionable; but he had an internal conviction
that scientific truths could be reconciled with Scriptural, even though his own spiritual insight might
not be deep enough to show their accord. One of
the chief arguments of his priestly accusers seems to
have been, that Joshua commanded the sun to stand
still, and it obeyed him; and that *if the sun had not
been in motion, it could not have been commanded
to stand still!* Galileo replied that in the Bible
we read that the heavens are *solid,* and *polished
like a mirror of brass,* and that a man had only to
raise his eyes to see that this language could not be
interpreted literally. These and similar arguments

and quotations from sacred writ were silenced by the cry of "blasphemy!"

Guicardini says of him, that he wanted to reconcile what was irreconcilable, and adds, "The philosopher could not listen to advice. In vain all his friends bade him remain quiet; told him that it was impossible for him to combat so many enemies, and to triumph over so many rivals; that in the end he would only draw upon himself a thousand new unpleasantries. He listened to no one. He complained of being received coldly, and did not see that he himself tried the patience of the Cardinals by his importunities."

The French Chasles, one of his most recent biographers, writing in 1862, remarks: "A man of the world would not have attempted to wage war against calumny — like a child, to seize the lightning, and fight against the thunder. Galileo did not know that calumny is more terrible than thunder, the stratagems of envy more subtle than lighting — a thousand times more rapid, more impalpable, more destructive."

After Galileo's return to Florence, having published a work on hydrostatics, and another upon the spots on the sun, he resolved to go to Rome. This mission was a singular one, and betrays the self-reliant simplicity of his character. He was confident that his own eloquence, the precision of his calculations, the authority of his name, the weight of his genius, would win over the incredulous, would persuade the Pope, and convince all the members of the Sacred College.

In 1616, he obtained letters from the Grand Duke to the Cardinal Orsini.   Although the Cardinal received him warmly, the result of his mission proved his ignorance of the priesthood, and the fallacy of his hopes.   Far from making a convert of the Pope, Galileo was ordered to renounce the doctrine of the immovability of the sun, and the rotation of the earth ; not to teach it, and not to defend it, by word of mouth or in writing — except, indeed, as an hypothesis, and without affirming it.

He submitted, and left Rome.   For fifteen years, during the reign of the two Popes who preceded Urban VIII., he preserved the silence thus arbitrarily imposed upon him.

Such was his dread of being thought a heretic, that he said he preferred death, and induced Cardinal Bellarmin to publish a certificate of his (Galileo's) belief.

In 1623, Cardinal Maffeo Barberini was made Pope Urban VIII.   He had a great affection for the illustrious astronomer, and Galileo revelled in the hope that this new Pope would be in favor of the doctrine of Copernicus, and that through him the truth might be established. He dedicated to him his work on the comets, and, depending upon the Pope's protection, wrote his celebrated dialogue on the systems of Ptolemy and Copernicus.

This book, when it was published in Florence in 1632, contained a very remarkable engraving. A vast sea is represented, bearing vessels ready to sail. Three philosophers standing on the sea-shore are discussing the movement of the world, and the revolutions of the spheres. One is Sagredo, the Spaniard. One wears the Venetian costume — it is Salviati of Venice. These were two real personages, whom Galileo knew and loved, and who had openly accepted his doctrines. Sagredo proves by his philosophical arguments, and Salviati by mathematical deductions, the principles of Copernicus. The antagonist they are endeavoring to convince stands between the two philosophers. He is robed in Oriental draperies, and wears an Eastern turban. It is Simplicio, a man of past ages — the partisan of Ptolemy, and the advocate of ideas rendered respectable by the sanction of one's forefathers — a man who defends tradition, who declares that received doctrines and axioms content him, that appearances are all-sufficient for him, that the abyss into which new thinkers and discoverers are plunging, terrify him.

As confident as though he had met with no rebuff, Galileo once more set out for Rome. His chief object was to obtain permission to publish this work. After a delay of two months, during which the manuscript had been abundantly pruned by Fra Niccolo Riccardi, and by Père Visconti the mathematician, Galileo was allowed to return to Florence, to publish his book.

But his implacable enemies seized upon this very work for his destruction. They represented to Pope Urban VIII. that it was a personal attack upon himself—that Simplicio was intended for a portrait, or rather a caricature, of His Holiness. The Pope was highly incensed at the bare suggestion that his *protégé* dared to turn him into ridicule. Galileo was at once summoned to Rome. At first he was allowed to reside with the Tuscan ambassador, but not to leave the house; afterwards, he was imprisoned for several days, by order of the Inquisition. He was examined on the subject of his book, and proved that he had received permission for its publication. It is said that he fell upon his knees before the tribunal of Cardinals, imploring them not to pronounce him a heretic; for he was a good Catholic, and would remain one in spite of the whole

world.   He added that, if the book was condemned
to be burned, he himself would cast it in the flames,
on condition that he was informed upon what ground
such a sentence was passed.   Then he read aloud
the adjuration which had been prepared for him by
the friar Frenzuola, his bitter enemy, and the favorite of the Pope.   This Frenzuola, who aspired to
be the best military architect of that age, hated
Galileo for not having ranked him above Michel
Angelo, and, in spite of Galileo's denial, so thoroughly persuaded the Pope that Simplicio was designed as his portrait, that he never forgave the
astronomer.

The sale of the book was suspended, but Galileo
was allowed to return to Florence.

On the 23d of September, 1632, Galileo was
again cited to appear in Rome before the Inquisition.   In vain the ambassador Niccolini showed the
certificates of Galileo's physicians, affirming that he
was suffering from a malady which prevented his
travelling — in vain the cardinals Antonio Barberini
and Ginetti appealed to the Pope in Galileo's behalf: the answer was that Galileo's presence could
not be dispensed with, and that a litter would be
prepared for his removal.

On the 11th of January, 1633, he received a final
summons.   He was seventy years of age, and was

becoming very infirm; he dreaded the fatigues of the journey in his suffering and feeble condition; the plague was raging in cities through which he was forced to pass, and he had an unconquerable horror of infection; but there was no alternative, and he was compelled to set out on a journey which then occupied twenty-five days, though it is now accomplished in almost as many hours.

On reaching Rome he was lodged, as before, in the palace of the Tuscan ambassador, but soon transferred to the prisons of the Inquisition.

His trial commenced on the 12th of April. There is no proof that he was put to the torture, though it has often been asserted. It is recorded that with tears he implored the mercy of his judges; he was, nevertheless, condemned to the stake. The terrible alternative of Death, or a solemn, final recantation of assertions which he knew to be unquestionable truths, was left him. The struggle in his spirit must have been bitter, and the injustice of his judges could hardly have galled him more than their perverse ignorance. But life was sweet, even to the great philosopher, who could hardly have been supposed to fear death, and who must have felt within himself the consciousness that existence had been bestowed upon him that Science might make gigantic strides through his agency. He decided to go

through the *form* of recantation. This ceremony
required him to kneel and place one hand upon the
Bible, and to utter these words, which were dictated
to him by a priest: "I abjure, curse, and detest
the error and heresy of the motion of the earth, and
promise that I will never more teach, verbally or in
writing, that the sun is the centre of the universe
and immovable, and that the earth is *not* the centre
of the universe and movable."

It is, however, related that after the compulsory
utterance of this gross falsehood, rising from his
knees he muttered, with a look of fierce defiance,
" *The earth moves, notwithstanding?* " It was
deemed wise by those who overheard this declara-
tion to ignore it, for the time being.

After his recantation, Galileo was for several
months imprisoned in his dwelling at Rome. He
wrote to the Pope, begging that he might be re-
leased, or assigned some other place of confinement.
The Pope commanded him to go to Sienna, and take
up his abode with the Archbishop Piccolomini. The
archbishop had a great affection for Galileo, but
was obliged to obey the order received from Rome,
and to keep him under close *surveillance;* he was
not even permitted to accompany the archbishop to
his summer villa.

Galileo pined for Florence, and again and again

prayed to be allowed to return to his villa on the hill D'Arcetri. Just as he had lost all hope, he received the Pope's permission, coupled with a command which made him virtually a prisoner within his own walls, and forbade the entrance of visitors.

His two daughters were nuns in the adjacent Convent of San Matteo — a Franciscan convent founded in 1269, now abolished. He was devotedly attached to them, especially to the elder, and in former times visited them frequently. During his trial at Rome, his favorite daughter fell into a profound melancholy, brought on by her fears for her father, and shortly after his return she died. Her illness had only lasted six days, and Galileo was overwhelmed by the suddenness of the blow. The second daughter now became her father's companion, and too soon his nurse; for his health was seriously impaired, and his sight failed more and more, until he became totally blind.

After his return to the villa he lived nine years.

Though his captivity was irksome, he could not have been very rigidly guarded, for we hear of his being surrounded by pupils, who listened with eagerness to his instructions, and it is recorded that Milton visited him. Milton, say Galileo's biographers, gained access to him either by eluding the vigilance of his jailors, or by forcing his way into his presence. Chasles thus sketches the memorable meeting :

"Picture those two noble forms — I know of nothing more touching than their contrast. Galileo is blind; the nun, his daughter, the sole child left to him, sustains his faltering steps, while with his stick in his hand he tries to find his way in the garden which he planted and loved. His finely shaped Italian head encircled by a crown of silvery locks; the grandeur of his forehead; the purity of his profile; the classic harmony of all his features, testify to his race and his mental powers; while the winning smile, the delicacy of coloring, the bland softness of his countenance, reveal the man not insensible to worldly pleasures and the charms of social life.

"The young Englishman is more grave. A severe simplicity characterizes his appearance. His costume is more *recherché ;* his long golden-brown hair falls in curls upon his shoulders, and harmonizes with his great, blue, contemplative eyes, his melancholy and thoughtful smile, and the freshness of his complexion, which neither sensuality nor violent passions have robbed of its youthful brilliancy.

"As the twain seat themselves together upon the summit of that hill, where Milton can view the entire range of Florence, her marble palaces, her cupolas, her steeple clocks, her bridges, beneath which glides the Arno, what were his thoughts? Had he any pre-vision of his future destiny, and of that of England? Did some inner voice tell him that he would one day be celebrated like Galileo, blind like him, like him condemned to spend his last days in solitude, and like him misunderstood or calumniated by his contemporaries? And yet happier than he is, for Milton was destined to leave be hind him the picture of a green and proud old age."

It is not known to a certainty at what precise period these two celebrities met, but Chasles thinks that it was probably in 1638.

Towards the close of Galileo's life his persecutions were redoubled. Every conceivable obstacle was thrown in the way of the circulation of his works, and his relations with the outer world, already so limited, were narrowed more and more. The Inquisitor of Florence was ordered by the Pope to visit the captive from time to time, and assure himself that he was humble and very melancholy. And his cruel sufferings were heightened, says Chasles, " by the consciousness of his own moral feebleness, by remorse for his vain artifices and useless concessions, and the barren result of his long humility." For, he adds, " This Italian, half a Greek, sublime revealer of the mysteries of the starry firmament;

genius which preceded Newton, followed Bacon, proclaimed Descartes — was not a hero of moral courage : he was an illuminated genius!"

Men wrote and printed what they pleased against Galileo; he was forbidden to deny their assertions, to reply at all. And yet, during this period of blindness and captivity, he wrote and confided to the hands of a faithful friend the treatise which at a later period enabled Sir Isaac Newton to deduce the attraction of gravitation from the fall of an apple.

Tenderly watched over by his daughter, Galileo died on the 9th of January, 1642, in his seventy-ninth year. Newton was born at the close of the same year.

The celebrated Church of Santa Croce, the Florentine Westminster, is graced by an imposing monument raised to the memory of the great and persecuted astronomer. When the body of Galileo was conveyed to this sepulchre, the forefinger and thumb of one of his hands were severed from the corpse, to be·kept as a memento.

CONVENT OF VALLOMBROSA.

KING VICTOR EMMANUEL has recently made a law to protect the hospitable monks of Vallombrosa, or, rather, to prevent their compulsory hospitality from being too largely abused.

The founders of the ancient monastery of Vallombrosa decreed that all travellers should be welcomed, lodged, and fed, free of charge, for three days. The object of this charitable provision was, doubtless, to secure rest and shelter to weary pilgrims bent on holy missions. The monastery soon became celebrated, and yearly increasing crowds thronged its ever-open doors. Though no remuneration, for most bounteous cheer, can be demanded, a compensation, dictated by the generosity of the guest, is always *expected* — not, however, always *received*. Holiday people, from the neighboring towns have trespassed, in such large numbers, upon the liberal hospitality of the monks, that in the summer of 1865 they prayed the king to devise some method which would guard them against imposition, without violating the rules of their Order. The king's ingenuity must have been severely taxed. Finally he announced that no visitor could be received at Vallombrosa, unless he presented himself furnished with a passport. Regular tourists and strangers, who form that portion of the community from whom the monks are certain of remuneration, are still welcomed; while the Italian pleasure-seekers of the neighborhood, who have no need of passports (and carry no purses), are excluded by the royal edict.

This law inevitably created discontent. On several occasions excursionists have only been informed of its existence at the doors of the convent, and have wrathfully demanded admission, and caused such a disturbance, that the monks were compelled to summon military aid for their protection.

Vallombrosa is a corruption of the original name, *Valle Ambrosa — Shaded Valley.* In 1060 this lovely locality took the name of *Aqua Bella — Beautiful Water.*

Some of the most renowned poets have commemorated their visits to Vallombrosa. Ariosto and Milton have left their footprints in the "Shaded Valley" and by the "Beautiful Water."

Aurora Leigh, looking with disappointed eyes upon the peaceful, cultivated landscapes of Eng-

land, and contrasting them with the wildly picturesque scenery of her beloved Italy, says :

<blockquote>
"Not my chestnut woods
Of Vallombrosa, cleaving by the spurs
To the precipices.   Not my headlong leaps
Of water, that cry out for joy, or fear,
In leaping through the palpitating pines,
Like a white soul, tossed out to eternity
With thrills of time upon it.   Not, indeed,
My multitudinous mountains, sitting in
The magic circle, with the mutual touch
Electric, panting from their full, deep hearts
Beneath the influent heavens, and waiting for
Communion and commission."
</blockquote>

According to San Giovanni da Ghitigliano, who
writes from the solitary cell he had made for himself at Vallombrosa, towards the close of the fourth
century, the "Shaded Valley" was, at that period,
a wild forest, infested by noxious serpents and
beasts of prey.   It has now bloomed into an Eden.

Vallombrosa is twenty English miles from Florence.   After reaching the village of Pelago, which
lies four or five miles below the monastery, the
rest of the journey must be made on foot, in the
saddle, or in a sort of rude wicker basket, placed on
sledges, and drawn by oxen.   Ladies are usually
consigned to this extraordinary conveyance, and
learn, to their amazement, what an amount of jolting
and bouncing feminine humanity can endure un-
fractured.

The road follows the course of the mountain torrent, but has no particular interest until it reaches a grove of superb pine-trees, whose sombre branches meet in irregular arches overhead. Further on, the traveller is suddenly charmed by what appears to be a noble English park — verdant lawns and fertile meadows, pasture grounds, alive with herds of cattle, small lakes, used as trout preserves, and the whole girdled in by magnificent forests of chestnut, beech, and oak. The herbage is remarkable for its unfolding verdure, and even in winter retains the vernal freshness imparted by the moisture of the mountain streams.

The convent is of massive structure, and forms a quadrangle, with vast paved courts and high towers. It covers as much ground as a small village. In times of war the gates are closed, and the hospitable monastery is transformed into a redoubtable fortress.

The refectory accommodates two hundred persons. The extensive library contains many valuable manuscripts and rare volumes. The chapels and spacious halls are embellished by fine paintings.

The front windows of the convent command the whole valley of the Arno, to Florence — the hills above Lucca and the Carrara mountains rising grandly in the distance.

Male visitors only are received into the convent.

About a hundred yards from its principal entrance stands a rude, dilapidated *Albergo.* This is styled the *Foresteria,* and here the gentler sex are lodged. A monk, who is selected for this especial duty, superintends their entertainment. The holy Brother who holds the office at this moment is remarkably handsome and conversable, and not particularly monastic in his deportment; but he could not occupy so agreeable a position until his fitness and reliability had been well tested.

The doors of the convent are every morning surrounded by a crowd of needy peasants, women and children, who come to receive their breakfast from the charitable hands of the monks.

Half way up the steep declivity which rises in the rear of the monastery, upon a projecting cliff, stands a small white building, with an untended and weed-grown garden, oddly styled the *Paradisino.* This "*little Paradise*" is used as a hermitage by the most holy of the monks; and their solitary meditations not unfrequently induce the state of semi-trance called *ecstasy.*

The Monastery of Vallombrosa was founded in the eleventh century, by Giovanni Gualberto. He was the son of the Lord Petroio, in Val-di-pesa. His family was one of the noblest, the richest, the most powerful in Florence. His history is very remarkable.

At eighteen years of age he was a gay cavalier, wholly absorbed in worldly and sensual pleasures. At this period his beloved brother Hubert was killed in a quarrel by a young nobleman. "*A life for a life*" was the cruel creed of the cavaliers of those days. Not alone Giovanni's rage and grief, but his code of honor, impelled him to vengeance, and he resolved to take the life of the assassin.

One Good-Friday morning he went forth, clad in armor, and followed by his retainers, to attend mass at San Miniato al Monte. Passing through the narrow road that leads to the Basilica of San Miniato, he unexpectedly encountered the murderer of his brother! The latter was unarmed and alone. The adversaries stood face to face. The fiery Giovanni drew his sword, and at this signal the swords of his followers flashed from their scabbards. Giovanni was in the act of rushing upon his foe, when the culprit threw himself at the avenger's feet, extended his arms in the form of a cross, and, in the name of that merciful Saviour who, upon the day which they were both celebrating, died upon the cross, and pardoned sinners in dying, supplicated Giovanni to spare his live and pardon his crime. Giovanni paused — in his soul there was a fierce, brief struggle between mercy and revenge; but compassion prevailed. With a grand impulse of pardoning generosity, he sheathed his sword, stretched out his arms, and said, "Thou hast slain my brother: be thou a brother to me, in his stead, if thou canst!"

Filled with contrition, his adversary flung himself, weeping, into Giovanni's arms, bewailing his deed of blood, and again and again declaring his unworthiness to receive that forgiveness which had been so nobly and promptly granted.

This incident is commemorated by a fresco, placed in a tabernacle on the wall, by the roadside, upon the very spot where it occurred.

Giovanni, after embracing and comforting his foe, led him to the Church of *San Miniato*, whither he was bending his steps. The legend says that when the reconciled cavaliers knelt before the crucifix, the lips of the Saviour smiled upon Giovanni, and the head bowed in approbation.

Giovanni was so much overcome by this miraculous manifestation, that he forthwith renounced the world and joined the Fraternity of *San Miniato.* Here he led so exemplary a life, that when the Abbot died the monks proposed, although he was only twenty-three years of age, to elect him as their head; but he declined the distinction, upon the plea of his youth.

At a later period he retired to the solitude of Vallombrosa, and there built himself a small cell beside those of the two hermit monks who had made that wild forest their abode. This trio formed the nucleus from which sprang the Holy Order of Vallombrosa.

The miraculous token vouchsafed Giovanni became widely known, and crowds flocked to see him, to receive his pious counsels and his blessing. Some even assumed his rude garb, and bore him company.

Emperors and nobles poured in their treasures, to establish a community which boasted a founder so saintlike. The monastery became very wealthy through these endowments. The Countess Matilda was one of the most lavish in her benefactions.

Victor the Second conferred on San Giovanni Gualberto the title of Abbot General of the Order. He was then seventy-two years of age, but his humility prevented his ever assuming the robes of his office. He waged uncompromising war against the corruptions of the age, and succeeded in abolishing many abuses.

He died in 1073, eighty-eight years of age, after having passed seventy years in religious seclusion.

The present extensive buildings of the monastery were erected in 1637.

For a long period the monks of Vallombrosa strove in vain to obtain possession of the crucifix from which Giovanni affirmed that the Saviour had bowed his head, in token of heavenly approbation. The monks of *San Miniato* clamored against this demand of the brethren of Vallombrosa. This crucifix had become one of the most valuable possessions of San Miniato, and drew crowds to the church. Finally, Cosimo III., over whom the monks of Vallombrosa possessed great influence, prevailed upon the Fraternity of San Miniato to consent to the temporary removal of the cross to the Eighth Chapel of the Church of *Santa Trinita*, and to wait until the proper authorities could decide to which fraternity it ought to belong. No satisfactory decision was ever given, for the crucifix, to this day, remains at *Santa Trinita.*

Tradition declares that Giovanni Gualberto performed numerous miracles, and there is a famous well, near the sacristy of the Church of San Giovanni, in the *Piazza Santa Trinita,* the waters of which, having been blessed by the relics of this saint, are said to have effected wonderful cures when a malignant fever ravaged Florence in 1580.

In the Fifteenth Chapel of this Church there is a painting by Francisco Corsi, representing San

Giovanni Gualberto in the act of pardoning the murderer of his brother.

Banquets are given in the Monastery of Vallombrosa upon certain festivals, and at the same time a sort of rural fair is held. The peasants assemble on the green sward before the convent, and sing improvised verses to popular airs. On the *Festa of the Assunta* the monks present several poor young girls, whose blameless conduct has entitled them to reward, with a small dowry, which enables them to marry.

The celebrated Monastery of *Camaldoli* is about ten miles distant from Vallombrosa. It is situated on a rocky slope of the Apennines; the adjacent mountains are bleak and barren; but the region about *Camaldoli* is an oasis of fertile and picturesque loveliness.

The brethren of *Camaldoli* are a branch of the great Carthusian Order, and own a vast and productive territory — well-stocked dairy farms, extensive meadows, highly cultivated fields, and forests which produce, it is said, the finest timber in the world.

There is a sort of penal branch attached to this Institution, called the *Sagro Eremo*, or *Holy Hermitage !* This convent is located amid pine forests, on the very topmost height of the Apennines. From this altitude both the Adriatic and Mediterranean

seas are visible.   The climate is one endless winter.
The church is encompassed by small, rude, isolated
huts, and their inmates are essentially hermits.
The discipline is very rigid.   The monks hold no
communion with each other; speech is forbidden !
they have no life in common.   His scanty allowance
of bread and vegetables is passed to each monk
through a trap-door, which opens from the wall into
his cell.   Twice only, in the year, animal food is
supplied.   The sound of the human voice is never
heard, except in religious exercises in the chapel.
The monks are summoned to prayers seven times in
every twenty-four hours.

Two luxuries alone are permitted them, but it
is said they rarely avail themselves of either.   One
is access to a large library of historical and theolog-
ical works, from which they are allowed to select
books ; the other is a small garden, attached to
each hut, which they are at liberty to cultivate.
But the books remain unopened, and weeds possess
the neglected earth, which might be embellished by
hardy flowers.

The community of the *Holy Hermitage* is com
posed of three classes of monks — novices, who must
prove their fitness for the monastic life by two
years' residence at the *Sagro Eremo*, before they
are permitted to take their place in the more agree-

able monastery of *Camaldoli;* monks, who are
sent to the *Eremo* from *Camaldoli,* for a certain
period, as a punishment for the transgression of
some of the rules of their Order; and men who
come voluntarily to this place of penance, hoping
to atone for great crimes, or to deserve great future
happiness, by the joyless rigor of their lives upon
earth.

It is in the chapel alone that the members of the
community meet, and there the visitor may see one
of their commonest penances. It consists in prostration at the foot of the alter, the arms extended to
form the figure of a cross, and the forehead struck
violently against the marble steps. This act is often
performed several times by the same penitent during a single service.

There are two or three high festivals in the year,
upon which the monks are permitted to converse
and eat together, and some slight addition is made
to their bread and vegetables; but there are monks
who never avail themselves of this indulgence —
who never change their diet, and whose voices have
never been heard in those walls, except in the offices
of the choir. This rigid fasting and meditation is
said to produce the most seraphic visions, the
records of which are preserved in the archives of
the *Sagro Eremo.*

Not to so ascetic an Order belonged the jolly monks who invented the game by us known as that of "*Domino.*" M. Amedeo de Ponthien gives us its origin. He says that in the sixth century, in a Convent of Benedictine Brothers, two monks, Fra Oremo and Fra Giacomo, were condemned to do penance in the same cell. To wile away the tedious hours, they contrived a game, to be played with small square stones, upon which they had ingeniously made certain black marks, representing various combinations. But, as they were aware that the Abbot was in the habit of making his round, at stated times, in the corridor of the cells, they hit upon the plan of chanting at short intervals, in a loud voice, "*Dixit, Dominus Domino,*" to make the Abbot believe that they were engaged in their orisons. This game, we are told, was the game of *Domino,* which took its name from the last, and upon which they paused to play.

Florence and its Bridges, as seen from the Height of "San Miniato."—*Page* 107.

FLORENTINE BRIDGES.

Among the most remarkable and the most picturesque features of Florence are its old historic bridges, arching themselves over the Arno, as it noiselessly steals through the city — bridges that have witnessed many memorable scenes, and have been again and again swept away, when the mountain torrents swelled the quiet-looking stream to overflowing, and again and again rebuilt, with ever-increasing strength and beauty.

The bridge farthest to the east is called the *Ponte alle Grazie*, or *di Rubaconté*. This last name it received in honor of the Milanese *Podestà Rubaconté*, who laid the foundation stone, and to whom the city of Florence was in various ways indebted. The first appellation it derives from a little chapel at the foot of the bridge, dedicated to Santa Maria delle Grazie.

The bridge was built by Lapo, father of the celebrated Arnolfo.

It was at the foot of this bridge, that in 1273 the two

discordant factions styled *Ghibellines* and *Guelphs,* through the mediation of Gregory X., met, and with great solemnity concluded a peace, which was to last until death.

Pope Gregory X., in company with the French King, Charles, and with Baldwin of Flanders, chanced to pass through Florence, on their way from Rome to Lyons, where they were to hold a council. They were highly delighted with the fair city of Florence, and resolved to pass the summer there. The Pope greatly lamented the bitter feud which existed between the proud Ghibellines and the fiery Guelphs, and noticed the constant injuries which the beautiful city sustained through the strife. (The Ghibellines are the party in favor of the Empire as opposed to the Church, and the Guelphs in favor of the Church as opposed to the Empire.) Pope Gregory, not questioning his power, made up his mind to put a sudden end to these unseemly dissensions. The Ghibelline leaders were then in exile, and he ordered that they should return, and make peace with the Guelphs. The Pontiff had a huge scaffolding of wood erected at the foot of the *Ponte alle Grazie,* and here, on the second day of July, 1273, all the dignitaries were seated, with the Pope in the centre. The Florentine people congregated in the dry bed of the Arno. The Pope sol emnly addressed the assembled multitude, and decreed that the Ghibellines and the Guelphs should become friends forevermore, under pain of excommunication to whoever should not obey the order. He made the Syndics of each party, who were doubtless more inclined to tear each other to pieces than to embrace, publicly kiss one another on the mouth, and give bail and hostages.

The ceremony was performed with all due solemnity; but the forevermore during which the peace thus forcibly concluded was to last, represented a period of four days! After this brief respite the feud broke out with fresh fury, and raged more violently than ever.

The incensed Pope retired immediately from Florence, and kept his word by excommunicating the whole city. Under this interdict Florence remained, with the exception of a short interval, for three years. The only removal of the excommunication was owing to a somewhat singular circumstance. The Pope, in returning from Lyons to Rome, intended to cross the Arno above the city of Florence, but the river was so much swollen that the passage of a ferry-boat was impossible. The Pope could not place his holy foot in a city that was excommunicated — for his presence was supposed to be synonymous with blessings. There was no alternative but to take off the interdict before he entered the gates. As he traversed the streets he dispensed his blessings according to established custom, but when he passed out of the opposite gate he immediately *took back all the blessings*, so profusely showered, and fulminated the excommunication anew.

In one of the small houses, standing on a pier of the bridge, the poet Menzini was born, and in another the Franciscan monk, Beato Tommaso dei Bellaci.

The *Ponte Vecchio* (or jewellers' bridge, as it is often called) is lined by shops of jewellers, goldsmiths, and other workers in metal. This bridge is said to be built on Etruscan piers. It was carried away by a flood in 1177 — rebuilt, and again swept away in 1333. It was rebuilt by Taddeo Gaddi in 1335. An inscription beneath one of the arches commemorates the fact. The officers of the *Torre*, or Towers, presided at its reconstruction, and the arms of the Torre, sculptured under the Loggia, or open part of the bridge, are mingled with those of the Republic.

Upon this bridge, in 1420, was signed the treaty of peace between Pope Martin V., and Fortebraccio, Lord of Pisa.

It was this Pope Martin who, on the year previous, had evinced his gratitude to the city of Florence for its hospitality, by presenting the *Signoria* with a golden Rose — a very signal honor. The presentation of a Rose of gold upon Easter Sunday, by the Roman Pontiff, to a prince or potentate who has won his favor, is a very ancient custom. Cambri describes the Rose as "a golden bough, with leaves of gold, very fine, and on it nine roses, and one bud above the nine; and inside there was musk, and myrrh, and balsam."

Upon Easter Sunday, second of April, 1419, when Pope Martin presented Florence with his Rose, the Gonfaloniere (Mayor), Bernardo di Costello, was prevented by a serious illness from receiving the much-prized offering. Taddeo Gherardini, chairman of the Signoria, for that day occupied *Bernardo's* place; and from that time his family was called Gherardini della Rosa. After the Pope had placed the Rose in the hands of Messer Taddeo Gherardini, the Pontiff came out on the Piazza Santa Maria Novella with thirteen cardinals, and the members of the Signoria. They all, the Pope excepted, mounted their horses, and eleven cardinals led the way; then came Messer Taddeo, with his Rose; two cardinals followed him, and the *Signoria* closed the procession; the horsemen passed through all the principal streets, and then returned to the Palazzo Vecchio. The Rose was ceremoniously placed in the chapel of the palace, where it remains to the present day.

In one of the houses upon the *Vonte Vecchio*, the poet Ariosto was entertained, for six months, by Cavaliere Niccolo Vespucci, on the occasion of the feast of St. John and the election of Leo X. ; and here the poet first saw *Alessandra Bennucci*, widow of *Tito Strozzi*, and fell in love with her. The correspondence between this lady and the poet lasted uninterrupted until her death in 1532, and she appears to have reciprocated his attachment.

Above the shops which line the bridge was a gallery ingeniously uniting *Palazza Pitti* to the galleria degli Uffizi, and the Palazzo Vecchio, built by Cosimo I.

It was at the foot of this bridge that the gallant young bridegroom, *Buondelmonte*, coming from his nuptials, was waylaid by the outraged relatives of a fair lady he had deserted. He was slain at the base of the statue of Mars. This statue was afterwards removed from its place near the bridge, on account, it is said, of the sad associations to which it was forever linked.

The *Ponte à Santa Trinità* is by far the most beautiful of the bridges. The former bridges, which occupied the site of the present one, have frequently been swept away. The last bridge was constructed by Bartolommeo Ammanati, architect to the Grand Duke, Cosimo I. It was finished in 1569. From its incomparable lightness and elegance, it was thought too fragile to sustain great weights; and heavily laden wagons were prohibited by the authorities from crossing. Ammanati, highly indignant at being supposed so unskilful as to build a bridge which was insecure, ordered an immense car to be filled with stones. The car was so ponderous, that it could with difficulty be drawn by six strong horses. Upon these stones the architect himself mounted, and was drawn to the centre of the bridge. Here he remained for several hours, discoursing with the people from his throne of stones, and practically convincing the Florentines of their error, and of the injustice they had done him. Yet one hundred and fifty years passed, ere carriages were allowed by the Grand Duke to pass over it.

An inscription cut in the stone of this bridge records the name of a brave Frenchman, who, when the Arno was swollen, and rushing onward with a fierce current, threw himself into the river to save a poor Florentine artisan, and though the unfortunate man's leg was broken, rescued him, at the imminent risk of his own life, and restored him to his family.

The angles of the bridge are adorned by statues

of the four seasons. The one representing winter, by *Taddeo Landini,* is considered the finest.

The *Ponte alla Carrajà* is said to have been the second that was built, and it was called *Nuovo Ponte,* in contradistinction to the *Ponte Vecchio.* The architect was Lapo. It was first erected in 1218, and swept away by a flood in 1269.

A most appalling catastrophe imparts great interest to this bridge. It was an ancient custom in Florence to celebrate the first weeks in May by superb pageants. This *Ponto alla Carrajà* was the favorite bridge for the exhibition of spectacles to the people. The different parties and companies of Florence vied with each other to gain the palm for grandeur and originality of display.

In the year 1304, the company *San Frediano* resolved to offer a magnificent May-day *fête* to the Cardinal *Niccolo da Prato,* who was then visiting Florence. T. A. Trollope, in his "Commonwealth of Florence," quaintly remarks that they wished to invent a *fête* "which should be magnificent, and at the same time *especially adapted* to the sacred character of the guest whom they wished to honor. So it was determined to regale the dignified Dominican Cardinal with a representation of Hell, and the torments of the damned, depicted *to the life.*"

The company sent around the city a band of

musicians and a herald, to announce that whoever wanted to have news of the other world, must come to the *Ponte alla Carrajà*. The bridge was at that time constructed of wood. The painter *Buffal-macco* directed the spectacle. A quantity of artificial fire, of various colors, was employed to lend splendor and reality to the performance. The infernal regions were represented upon the Arno. The river was covered with rafts and barges, peopled with demons, rushing about, amidst flames, groaning, shrieking, yelling, and inflicting torment upon "naked souls;" these "naked souls" of the condemned being made manifest by "naked bodies." We quote Trollope's description of what ensued: "The scene was at its height, and the interest and satisfaction of the beholders proportionably intense, when all at once the bridge, burthened beyond its strength by the vast crowd of spectators, fell with a crash into the hell beneath, overwhelming the devils and their victims and the crowd of gazers in one common ruin, of an indescribable mass of inextricable confusion! What with the fall, and the injuries by the timbers of the ruined bridge, and drowning in the water, and crushing one another, few either of the actors or spectators of the scene escaped with their lives."

It is said that there was hardly a family in Florence which did not lose a relative by this catastrophe. The historian Villani coolly observes that *"they saw hell much nearer than they intended."*

The painter Buffalmacco happily escaped. He had left the bridge a few moments before the accident, to procure something needful to the show.

It is related that Dante was present at this spectacle, and that he there first conceived his idea of the *Inferno.*

Not far from the *Ponte alla Carrajá* stands the house where *Amerigo Vespucci* was born. A tablet over the front of the dwelling bears an inscription recording the fact.

In 1304 the *Ponte alla Carrajá* was first built throughout with stone. In 1333 it was again entirely destroyed by the overflow of the Arno. It was then rebuilt by the architect Fra Giovanni di Campi in its present form, except that Ammanati, in 1557, rebuilt two of the arches, which had been carried away.

Every year, on the festival of San Giovanni, patron saint of Florence, the most splendid fireworks are exhibited from this bridge, and the Arno is covered with barges containing bands of music. The fireworks which we witnessed there in 1865 were superb beyond description; they were literally pictures painted in flashes of colored fire.

Florence has now added to her old historic bridges two modern suspension bridges, the *Ponte San Fernando* and the *Ponte San Leopoldo*. They were constructed by a French engineer, and completed in 1837, but the furious little Arno proved too strong to be resisted by one of them. The bridge above the *Ponte alle Grazie* was swept away in November, 1844, and rebuilt in 1853.

As we stand upon any one of these bridges, and watch the slender stream, gliding through the street, and winding through richly green valleys, and we lift up our eyes to palaces, towers, and churches singularly imposing in their individuality, and then to San Miniato, to *Fiesole*, and Bellosguardo, to the background formed by the stately Vallombrosan hills and the purple peaks of the Carrara mountains, we are forced to admit that it is the position of those bridges, and the landscape, replete with rare and varied loveliness which they command, that redeems the narrow little Arno from insignificance, and imparts to it the pictorial aspect for which it is celebrated.

DANTE.

July 3, 1865.

Is Dante to be allowed to rest at last? Are we to have any rest from Dante? Italy has been Dante mad for a couple of months. Dante's glorification has been the signal for the most brilliant extravagance and superb festivity. After a lapse of six centuries, a frantic desire to pay homage to their great poet has suddenly stirred the pulses of the Italian people into jubilant enthusiasm.

We do not venture upon the suggestion on this side of the ocean, but we are almost brave enough to whisper to our friends on the other, that although it is just possible a genuine and intense appreciation of the writings and character and political services of Dante may have made the nation seize with such wild avidity upon the opportunity to do him honor, it is even more probable that the Italian holiday-loving heart was simply overjoyed to snatch at any excuse for a series of *fêtes*.

The three days' solemnities at Ravenna have just

(118)

terminated. Dante's recovered bones have been finally sepulchred with impressive pomp and ceremony. Their discovery, made a little more than a month ago, is somewhat singular.

The exiled Dante died at Ravenna, September 14th, 1321. His unquiet bones seem to have passed through extraordinary vicissitudes. A few years after Dante's death, when Cardinal Bertrando del Pogetto, moved by pious wrath, determined that the poet's remains should be burned as those of a heretic, they were stolen by some Franciscan friars. Tradition says they were restored to their original resting-place when the danger was over. In 1519 the Florentines supplicated Pope Leo X. to have the poet's venerated bones brought to Florence, Dante's birth-place, as Michael Angelo had offered to sculpture a sepulchre worthy to be their last receptacle. The people of Ravenna cried out against this demand, and the bones once more mysteriously disappeared. It is not definitely stated when or how they were restored, but since they were destined to vanish again, they must have been replaced. When Cardinal Corsi, in 1692, attempted to repair the chapel of Dante, the friars suspected that his object was to obtain possession of these valued relics, and once more they became invisible. Their repository was not again discovered until the 27th of May, 1865 —

just after the great Dante festival celebrated in Florence.

The municipality of Ravenna having approved of the programme for that festival, and wishing to do further honor to the poet, ordered that the chapel of Dante should be opened and repaired. The masons employed on the work found embedded in a wall, from which they had removed a few stones to fasten a pipe, a badly made firwood box. It was opened by them. An inscription within testified that the bones it contained were those of Dante, placed there by Friar Antonio Santi, 18th of October, 1677. The archives of the Franciscan College were examined, and a record of this act, made by Friar Antonio Santi, was found.

Here was a glorious occasion for another *"festa,"* and the 24th, 25th, and 26th of June were set apart for Dante's final obsequies. Military salutes, processions, bands of music, orations, and banquetings formed part of the ceremony.

The bones were carried to the temple of Bracciaforte, upon a white satin cushion, in a crystal urn covered with a white veil. When the veil was lifted, the Syndic of Ravenna made a touching address, and then placed a wreath upon the urn. A second wreath was offered by the Syndic of Florence. No priests were permitted to officiate. Their ire was very naturally excited, and they pronounced the whole proceeding sacrilegious.

The three days' national Dante festival in commemoration of the six hundredth anniversary of his birth, took place in Florence on the 14th, 15th, and 16th of May, 1865, and has never, it is said, been surpassed in magnificence — at least in Italy.

It will seem strange to our American readers that Sunday was the day upon which the festival commenced, but that sacred day is usually chosen by Italians as the fittest for a jubilee.

A colossal statue of Dante was to be inaugurated on the Piazza Santa Croce. The piazza was richly adorned with decorative paintings, illustrative of incidents in the life of the poet, garlands of laurel and flowers, trophies, banners, emblematical devices, and rich hangings. Indeed, the whole city was hung with flags, and upon those houses in which great celebrities have lived, or died, or were born, their names were inscribed, surrounded with garlands and trophies.

The procession was formed in the Piazza Santo Spirito at ten o'clock in the morning. Men and women marched bareheaded in the broad sunshine. Conspicuous among the most renowned moved the great Ristori, the most distinguished actress of Italy. She was arrayed in a flowing robe of gold colored silk, which swept the streets, and wore a crown of gold upon her stately head, with a long, rich white veil. Her noble carriage, her graceful, regal gait, and her handsome features, won general admiration. Salvini and Rossi, the two greatest of Italian actors, walked by her side. A superb banner, representative of the dramatic art, of which they each held a ribbon, was borne before them.

When the procession had assembled in the Piazza Santa Croce, the solemn bell of the Palazza Vecchio sounded; then followed superb music by the band of the National Guard. King Victor Emmanuel gave the signal for the unveiling of Pazzi's statue of Dante, and an oration was pronounced.

The statue is severely criticised on the one hand and highly praised on the other; but it is sufficient that Pazzi, the sculptor, is a native of Ravenna for him to excite the jealousy of the Florentines. It is said he has made Dante frowning upon ungrateful Florence. The King knighted Pazzi for his work.

In the evening, the whole city was illuminated with a dazzling brilliancy, of which no language can give an adequate conception. A triple row of lights gleamed along the whole length of the Arno, and reflected a blaze in the water. The bridges, the Pitti Palace, the Palazzo Vecchio, the Duomo,

Baptistry, Giotto's Campanila, were literally, in the language of Aurora Leigh,

"Drawn in fire."

All Florence, from its princes and potentates down to the lowest *contadini*, poured into the streets. The order and quiet preserved were wonderful. Great as was the crowd, there was no jostling, no pushing, no rudeness, no loud talking; the hum of low voices and the sound of music alone broke the stillness. The finest band and choir were to be heard in the Piazza Santa Croce.

Upon the second day, the celebration was continued in the Academy of Fine Arts. Several original poems on Dante were delivered, and Ristori read, with great effect, Victor Hugo's letter to the Mayor of Florence. A Dante concert was given in the evening at the Pagliano Theatre.

On the third and last day, the festivity began with a distribution of prizes to women of good conduct, on the Piazza Santa Croce.

During the day there was a *festa* for the populace, and mock tournament on the Cascine, and a boat-race on the Arno.

At night a ball for the people in the open air, under the Uffizi.

The *festa* closed with the most gorgeous *tableaux vivantes*, accompanied by music and recitation, at the Pagliano theatre. The magnificence and artistic beauty of these tableaux were unrivalled. They represented scenes from the works of Dante — chiefly from his *Divina Comedia.* The *Inferno,* with all its horrors and tortures, as Dante has fantastically described them, was illustrated by a series of pictures exhibited by a fiery red, electric light. *Purgatory,* with its milder suffering, was shown by a cold blue, electric light. But the electric light shed a golden blaze of glory when Heaven, with Dante led by Beatrice, amidst groups of angels and apostles, with the blue vault and bright stars, and fleecy clouds above them, were revealed.

The tableau of Francesca di Rimini was preceded by a recitation, powerfully given, by the great Ristori. Declamations by Salvini and Rossi preceded several of the tableaux.

It was a great source of pride and congratulation by the American visitors in Florence, that an exquisite translation of the Divina Comedia, by our own Longfellow, richly bound, was sent by the poet himself, through the Minister, Mr. Marsh, to the Mayor.

It is also gratifying to remember, that the full-length portrait of Dante, by Giotto, in the chapel of the palace of the Podesta, which, on an occasion of this kind, when the city swarmed with strangers, was an object of especial interest, might have still remained hidden by the coat of whitewash which had concealed it for generations, but for the energy of our countryman, Mr. R. H. Wilde, assisted by a few English and American gentlemen. The whitewash was, in some places, an inch thick, and it is not definitely known how long the portrait had worn this unseemly white veil.

The day before the festival instituted by the authorities commenced, it may be said to have been inaugurated at the " English Dramatic Drawing Room," by an admirable lecture delivered by Mr. Montgomery Stuart, correspondent of the London *Morning Post.*

The national ovation has caused Italy, we might almost say Europe, to be flooded with pamphlets, poems, sonnets, discourses, and books on Dante, his life and times. Certainly no poet ever won a more bounteous tribute of venerating admiration. We quote an illustrative passage from a highly interesting volume written by a Greek lady, noted for her beauty and talents, Madame Albana Mignaty. She says : " When we have granted to Dante his full share of weakness, passion, inconsistency, and even bitterness, enough remains of heroic strength, and of unquenchable ardor in the pursuit of virtue, to ensure Dante, our Tuscan father, the admiration of all ages, as the *Prince of Christian Poets*, and the foremost of all those who have sought to guide mankind through suffering and through faith to their eternal home."

Having given this quotation, we are bound to confess that we do belong to the number of Dante's worshippers. While we admit that he has claims to high rank as a poet; that he gave to Italy her language; that he united wonderful imagination to vast scientific knowledge and political wisdom; that, although he was a *dreamer*, he showed an acquaintance with scientific facts then supposed to be unknown, and which seemed prophecies as they were recorded by his pen; and while our deepest sympathy is excited by his misfortunes, and the harsh ingratitude which he received at the hands of those whom he had so largely benefited; while we grieve over his sad exile, his lonely wanderings — his poverty, which, he declares, caused him almost to live on alms; while we are moved by his yearnings for his native city, and his sad death at Ravenna — in short, while we admit his mighty genius and his heavy sorrows, we cannot feel that his character commands that amount of *veneration* which it so lavishly receives. He is called the most *Christian* of poets, the most high-minded and noble, and large-hearted of men, etc., etc. But this *Chris-*

tian poet cherished inveterate and deadly hatreds, wholly inconsistent with the teachings of Christianity, incompatible with the character of a Christian. And when he describes the *Inferno*, the *Christian* poet takes care to give all of his enemies a conspicuous place there, and to depict their tortures with savage triumph.

His egotism has scarcely a parallel in biography. He *himself*, *his* emotions, *his* aspirations, *his* adventures, *his* self-laudation, are constantly the themes of his muse.

He is called the *true lover Poet*, who has deified the passion of love in the style of his Beatrice. But what is the matter-of-fact history of that same passion? He had very little beyond a *bowing acquaintance* with his idolized Beatrice; indeed, her ceasing to salute him at one time affords the opportunity for a frantic burst of poetic agony.

He was nine years old when he first met Beatrice. She had just entered her ninth year. During the next nine years he only saw her by chance glimpses. In his "Vita Nuova" he thus describes their first meeting: "Nine times from the hour of my birth had the heaven of light returned, as it were, to the same point in the orbit, when the glorious lady of my thoughts appeared for the first time before my eyes. By many she was called Beatrice, by some

she was known by another name. She was then of
such an age that the starry heavens had moved the
twelfth part of a degree towards the earth during
her life time, so that she appeared to me about the
beginning of her ninth year, and I saw her about
the end of my ninth year. She appeared to me in
a dress of noble color, a subdued and becoming
blood-red, with a sash and ornaments suited to her
very youthful years. At that moment (I speak the
truth) the *spirit of life*, which dwells in the most
secret chamber of the heart, began to tremble so
violently as to be frightfully visible in the smallest
pulses of my body, and with faltering voice said
these words: 'Behold a God stronger than I, whose
coming will subdue me.'"

Of his second meeting he says, " When exactly so
many days had elapsed after the above described
apparition of this most noble lady as were necessary to complete nine whole years, it chanced that
on the last of those days this most admirable person
appeared to me in a dress of the purest white, between two noble ladies older than herself, and passing along the street she turned her eyes to the spot
where, trembling with fear, I stood, and with an in-
effable courtesy (which now has its reward in eter-
nity) saluted me in so striking a manner, that I
seemed to reach the very extreme of happiness.

The hour at which I received this most bewitching salutation was precisely the noon of the day, and as this was the first time that her words had reached my ears, the pleasure which I received was such that I quitted the company, as it were, in a state of intoxication, and, retiring to my solitary chamber, I sat down to meditate on this most courteous lady. During my meditation a sweet sleep came over me, in which appeared a wonderful vision."

The vision is minutely described, and is followed by his first love sonnet. When the father of Beatrice died, Dante's sympathy for her sorrow was so great that he fell ill, and on the ninth day of his indisposition he saw a vision of the death of Beatrice herself.

Nine was to him the most sacred of numbers, and when Beatrice dies he says, "According to the mode of reckoning in Italy, her blessed soul departed in the first hour of the ninth day of the month, and according to the computation in Syria, she died in the ninth month of the year, for the first month is their Tismin (Tizri), which is our October. And according to our calculations, she departed in that year of our calendar, that is, in the year of our Lord in which the perfect number has been *nine* times completed in the century in which she was born in the world, and she was a Christian of the thirteenth century. The following may be a reason why this number was so propitious to her : since, according to Ptolemy, and the belief throughout Christendom, there are nine stars which move, and according to the common belief, these stars have an influence on things here below, according to their positions — this number was propitious to her in giving it to be understood, that at the time of her generation all the nine morning stars were in the most perfect conjunction."

At Beatrice's death, his vehement anguish was so overpowering, that he addressed an extravagant letter to the " potentates of the earth," informing them that " the whole city of Florence was widowed by her loss."

But this is the *embroidered* side of the tapestry of his love history. The reverse does not altogether correspond.

Strange to say, we hear nothing of his ever having sought Beatrice in marriage, nor of his sufferings when, at the age of twenty, a bridal ring was placed upon her delicate finger by another hand.

After her death, which he so violently laments, he declares that he consecrates his whole life to her memory, and that he " hopes to speak of her as no woman was ever spoken of before ; " and somewhat later he bitterly reproaches himself (in " The Convinto ") because he is attracted to a certain lady by her compassionate looks and earnest sympathy for his grief. When he finds his thoughts turning too often to " the gentle stranger," he upbraids himself for the temporary solace, as though the pleasurable emotion were a crime.

Yet, in 1293, only three years after the death of Beatrice, he marries Gemma Donati, and in the course of time becomes the father of seven children. Surely this Gemma must have been one of the most patient, forbearing, and unjealous of womankind, for Dante continues to rave of his beloved Beatrice, and his writings continue to be full of his personal experiences; he continues to admit the reader into the inner sanctuary of his soul; he continues to

" Throw out acclamations of self-thinking, self-adoring,"

though poor Gemma and his *quiver* with the *seven arrows* are ignored. In the *Purgatorio* alone, *one* passing allusion is made to his family. All that was real and tangible had not the same actual existence to him as that which was ideal or visionary. The uncomplaining woman who sat by his hearth and cradled his children in her arms, had a less *positive existence* than the departed Beatrice, whom he could scarcely be said to have known — a proceeding which a prosaic friend of ours quaintly pronounces, "*poetic*, not *proper*."

Besides this, Boccaccio tells us that Beatrice was by no means the poet's only flame. One of the objects of his admiration has come down to us as Gentucca of Lucca, sometimes called Porgoletta; another is said to have dwelt among the green hills of the Casentino, and seems to have been beloved in spite of a *goître ;* and to each of these fair ones the " *true lover* " poet wrote impassioned sonnets.

He gave to his daughter the name of Beatrice, perhaps in remembrance of his first love, whom he wished the world to believe his *only love.* Of this daughter little is known. She was a nun in the convent at Ravenna at the time of her father's death. His wife he never saw after his exile.

After calling to mind these rather startling little biographical facts, are we not justified in saying, that, although Dante was a great genius, he was by no means the most *Christian* of poets, the noblest of men and the *truest* of lovers? Heaven defend the young maidens of the present generation from such a love! or the destined wives from such a husband!

FLORENTINE FEUDS.

SERRAVEZZA, Valley of the Apennines,
Near Florence, Aug. 22, 1865.

SOME of the most thrilling episodes in Florentine history are those which record the deadly feuds that separated illustrious families, or existed between the nobles and the people — feuds which lasted for centuries, and supplied the chronicler with an abundant treasury of romantic incidents.

The Ghibellines were the ancient nobility of Florence, and were opposed to the Guelphs, who were the representatives of the people. Their furious dissensions involved the Florentine republic in numerous sanguinary wars, threw the Government into confusion, and entailed on all classes a perplexing series of misfortunes.

The feud, which originated in a private quarrel between Buondelmonti and Tifonti, culminated in a fearfully tràgic catastrophe, and was most fatal and enduring in its consequences.

In 1215, the Order of Knighthood was conferred upon Mazzingno of the Mazzinghi. He gave a feast to celebrate an event which did him so much honor. Buondelmonte Buondelmonti, a young and gallant cavalier, noted for the attractions of his person and the fascination of his manners, was invited. An altercation arose between two of the guests, Uberti Infangati and Oddo Tifonti. The fiery Buondelmonti, ever ready to plunge into a quarrel, started up, and took sides with Infangati. His manner was so violent and his language so vehement, that Tifonti seized a plate from the convivial board and dashed it in his face. At this indignity all the guests sprang from their seats. The friends of Buondelmonti drew their daggers and rushed upon Tifonti. He must inevitably have lost his life had he not been defended and rescued by the cooler portion of the company. The host made an eloquent appeal to the excited young men, and finally succeeded in calming their ire and reconciling Tifonti and Buondelmonti to each other. They shook hands, and the guests reseated themselves at the banquet table. But it was feared that the reconciliation thus forced upon the cavaliers would not be permanent. To ensure its duration, a marriage was proposed between young Buondelmonti and the niece of Oddo Tifonti, of the noble family of Amedei. Buondelmonti was too courteous to refuse the proposition, although he had no preference for the young lady thus suddenly offered to him as a bride; to have declined her hand would have added a fresh insult to the one he had already given Tifonti. Preparations were forthwith made for a magnificent wedding.

When these tidings reached the ears of Madonna Aldruda, of the noble Donati family, she was filled with dismay. She had watched the young Buondelmonti from his childhood, and in her heart had selected him for the bridegroom of her beautiful daughter, just budding into womanhood. She could not resign herself to this sudden awakening from her brilliant dreams. At the hour when she knew Buondelmonti would pass her house, she stood in her doorway to salute him. The young cavalier reined in his steed when he saw her, and after she had greeted him with even more than wonted courtesy, she drew forward her lovely daughter, and presenting her to him, said, "*This have I kept for thee!*"

The impressionable youth was charmed by the modesty and beauty of the young maiden, and touched by the words of the mother. Prompted by an unreflecting impulse, he sprang from his horse, and taking the young girl by the hand, replied, "*I should be ungrateful to refuse your gift, lady,*" and entered the house. During this, his first interview with the fair damsel, he became so much en-amored, that he resolved to break his faith with the niece of Tifonti. He at once betrothed himself to the daughter of Madonna Aldruda Donati, and their nuptials took place without delay.

When Oddo Tifonti learned that the affianced husband of his niece had wedded a Donati, he vowed a terrible vengeance.

The enraged family of the forsaken lady met in council, and decided that Buondelmonti should be severely wounded and *maimed*, as the penalty of his inconstancy. But Mosca Lamberti deemed each punishment insufficient. "*This King has got a head!*" he ejaculated as he wrathfully arose to demand a sterner retribution. Then it was decided that Buondelmonti should suffer death.

Easter Sunday is celebrated by the Catholic Church as one of its holiest and grandest festivals. That was the day selected for the execution of Buondelmonti's sentence. He had been married one week. He rode gayly forth on that bright Easter Sunday, attired in a suit of pure white, and upon a white steed; his young bride herself had buckled on his sword. It may well be imagined with what loving pride the innocent girl watched the noble and handsome cavalier as he mounted his horse in his bridal garb. She was never more to look upon his living face!

He rode rapidly over the Ponte Vecchio (now the well-known Jeweller's bridge), but at the foot of the bridge received a blow upon his head, which hurled him from his horse. Oddo Tifonti then fell upon him, and with his own hands opened his enemy's veins, and savagely watched him bleed to death.

The tradition further says that his young bride was seized and placed in an open car, which held the bleeding body of her husband, and with his head laid upon her lap, the car was drawn through the streets of Florence to exhibit the vengeance which a noble and insulted family had taken upon a faithless cavalier.

The whole city took part in this quarrel. Of sixty-two Florentine noble families, thirty-nine became Guelphs or friends of the Buondelmonti, and the rest Ghibellines or partisans of the Amedei; and the two parties were ever after the most inveterate foes. Constant contentions, bloody frays, and even desperate wars sprang out of this unhappy division.

At a little later period, 1258, a most romantic incident gave an important place in history to another member of the Buondelmonti family — like his predecessor, a young and gallant cavalier.

Between the illustrious family of the Bardi (whose ancient mansion is still visible in the street of that name), and the family of the Buondelmonti a most implacable hereditary hatred had existed for generations.

Ippolito Buondelmonti, in his twenty-first year, is described as a golden-haired, blue-eyed, symmetrically proportioned youth, of noble presence. He had an enthusiastic temperament, a warm heart, and a character richly endowed with generous and manly attributes. Unfortunately, he fell in love with Dianora dei Bardi, the daughter of the bitterest enemy of his house. He had beheld her in church, and from that time haunted the street in which she lived. It is said that the apparent hopelessness of his passion caused him a dangerous illness. During this period his devoted mother succeeded in obtaining his confidence. Instead of reproaching her son for his weakness, and bidding him forget the young maiden to whom he had given his heart, she gave him most tender and womanly sympathy, and even bade him hope that the breach between the two contending families might be healed, and Dianora become his bride. Her words of consolation possessed a restorative power that acted like magic, and Ippolito recovered with a ra-

.pidity which astonished and perplexed his physicians.

Meantime the mother formed a plan which enabled the lovers to meet, upon the occasion of a great festival, given at Monticelli, the villa of one of her ancient friends. The hostess and mother even allowed the youthful couple an opportunity of conversing without witnesses. During that single interview Dianora was wooed and won by the enemy of her house. The happy pair were not only affianced, but the day of their marriage was fixed, and the manner in which Dianora was to be stolen from her father's house concerted. In ten days a priest and proper witnesses were to assemble in the chapel of the Servite convent of the Holy Trinity, at an altar belonging to the Buondelmonti. Ippolito was to let his lady love know that all was in readiness, by giving her a signal as he passed beneath her balcony on that day, at a certain hour; and in the dead of the night he was to climb to her chamber window, by means of the silken ladder, then greatly in vogue, and return with his bride.

At the hour agreed upon, the signal was duly given, and Dianora, very joyful at heart, withdrew, to wait for the coming night. Ippolito had made all his preparations, and having concealed his silken ladder within his cap, set out, soon after midnight, for the house of his betrothed. Just as he had passed the Ponte Vecchio, and entered the Via dei Bardi, he heard behind him the tramping feet of the *Bargello* and his men, the patrol, and seized with a sudden panic, imagined they were in pursuit of him. Instead of attempting to hide himself, which he could easily have done by slipping into some of the narrow streets, he fled down the *Via dei Bardi*, and thus attracted the attention of the patrol, who at once gave chase. His swift feet might still have given him a chance of escape, but his cap, with its betraying contents, fell off, and he stopped to recover the lost treasure, upon which his future happiness depended. That brief pause gave the patrol time to reach and capture him.

He was instantly thrown into prison. When he was questioned, instead of avowing the truth, which he thought might tarnish the fair name of his bride, he accused himself of being engaged in a housebreaking expedition, and confirmed his story by details which seemed to leave no doubt of its truth.

Outrages were very frequent in those days, and it was necessary that justice should be dealt out summarily. The Guelph magistrate, if he would conciliate the good-will of the people, must, perforce, exert the authority of the law as unhesitatingly over a patrician offender as over the meanest citizen. On the very morning after his capture, Ippolito Buondelmonti, proved guilty by his own confession, was condemned to be beheaded.

His courage, and his determination to preserve his secret, remained unshaken by this sentence. His mother was admitted to his prison, and by her prayers and tears strove to induce him to let her reveal the truth and declare the part she had herself taken in aiding his fatal expedition; but he withstood all her entreaties. He said he had but one wish, and that was to behold Dianora once more. He therefore charged his mother to go to the Bargello, and petition him to allow the procession which would conduct him to the place of execution to pass through the Via dei Bardi.

This petition was readily granted. Soon after dawn on the morrow the procession issued from the prison doors. It was composed of the *Bargello* and his pikemen; then a couple of priests walking on either side of the prisoner, and chanting the Penitential Psalms; then the headsman, with his bared axe on his shoulder; then more pikemen; and then a crowd of people, who volunteered their attendance, and joined in the chants as they walked.

Dianora, when she arose that day, to the great surprise of her maidens, arrayed herself in her most superb attire. The members of her family had all assembled on the balcony to see the procession pass, and to glory over the humiliation and punishment of a detested Buondelmonti. Dianora did not join them until she heard that the procession was within sight.

Just as it passed in front of the balcony, and her lover raised his eyes to her face, to look the farewell he could not speak, Dianora, with pale cheeks and flashing eyes, suddenly stepped forward, and in a firm, clear voice, addressed the Bargello and the citizens of Florence. She bade them pause to listen to the testimony she had to give concerning their prisoner, Ippolito dei Buondelmonti.

Her proud relatives were too much amazed, too completely stunned by the suddenness of her action, to silence her.

The procession halted at her command. The crowd expressed the deepest emotion. When she again prepared to speak, some of the cavaliers of her family pressed forward to interfere, but she waved them back with a regal gesture, and turned to the Bargello and the citizens.

Then in rapid, but eloquent language, she told them that she would have been guilty of murder had she not spoken ; she declared that Ippolito was her affianced husband, in spite of the deadly feud which separated their families ; that he had generously allowed himself to be condemned as a mid-night robber to preserve her fair name unsullied; that on the night he was seized, in accordance with a plan they had laid, he was to have climbed to her chamber window to carry his betrothed to the altar; that she had hoped their union would end the wicked and senseless feud which existed between their houses; and she concluded by saying that she stood there an expectant bride, waiting for the fulfilment of her bridegroom's promise.

The crowd enthusiastically cheered the noble and courageous maiden, and would have yielded her Ippolito by force, if force had been needed. But he, fearing that she would only ruin herself and not save him, addressed her as one whom generous pity for his misfortune had caused to use this stratagem.

With a woman's ready wit, she interrupted his words, and reminded the crowd that a priest must have been engaged to perform the marriage cere-mony, and added that, as the testimony of that priest would prove her assertion, she demanded that a proclamation be made ordering him to appear.

It chanced that this very priest was one among the crowd. With great difficulty, he forced his way beneath the balcony, and testified that he had waited six hours in the Chapel of St. Agnes, having been ordered by Ippolito to be there for the celebration of the holy sacrament of marriage between himself and the noble lady, Dianora dei Bardi.

Then the delighted populace shouted tumultuously, "The prisoner is innocent! Long live the Buondelmonti! Long live the Bardi! A Buondelmonti and a Bardi! Ippolito and Dianora! Peace and union in Florence! To the palace! To the palace!"

The seat of the Republican Government was still called "*Palazzo Vecchio*"—on the *Piazza Grand Duca.*

The Bardi could not—*dared not*—gainsay the popular request. The rival families were forced together by a current too strong to be resisted. Ippolito was conducted by his guard to the palace. Dianora was escorted by her amazed but powerless relatives, and joined him there. Before an immense crowd, not made up of the people alone, but also composed of the principal families of Florence, Ippolito dei Buondelmonti and Dianora dei Bardi were united, and the feud between the rival houses was at an end.

Piazza Grand Duca, with Palazzo Vecchio and "Loggia di Lanzi."— *Page* 144.

FEUDS BETWEEN THE BIANCHI AND NERI.

THERE is nothing more remarkable in Florentine history than the endless feuds between the nobles and the people, or the nobles and one another, which for centuries distracted the Commonwealth, and occasioned not merely loss of individual life and property, and the demolition of so many stately palaces and other superb buildings, but culminated in fierce and protracted wars. And there is, perhaps, nothing in Florentine history more *singular* than the trivial first causes which gave rise to those battle-generating feuds.

T. A. Trollope, whose indefatigable researches have enabled him to produce the most complete history of the Florentine Commonwealth which has ever been written, says these divisions " must be attributed to some underlying cause, of longer and deeper significance than any to which they are attributed. A match falling into a powder barrel is in one sense the cause of all the wide-spread ruin that follows. But the destructive force which has been put into activity, had been previously prepared and stored up, without which the accidental match would have been harmless." Yet it is of interest to trace the often trivial circumstances which lighted the ready match and caused the explosion.

One of the most bloody encounters between the Florentines and their rivals, the Pisans, owed its origin to a lap-dog. The story runs thus: When the Emperor Frederick II. was crowned in Rome, 22d of March, 1220, all the Italian cities sent ambassadors to do honor to his Majesty. Between Florence and Pisa there always existed a bitter jealousy. As a matter of course, the rival cities selected men of the highest position in their community, and the ones most fitted to grace a royal festival.

A Roman Cardinal gave a dinner to the Florentine ambassadors and another to the Pisans. The banquet to the Florentines took place first. The Cardinal had a lap-dog of rare beauty, which gambolled around the feet of the ambassadors and won great admiration. One of the Florentine representatives was so much charmed that his Eminence presented him the little favorite, and begged that he would send for it whenever he pleased.

The next day, the Pisan ambassadors dined with

the Cardinal. The dog had not yet been claimed by the Florentine ambassador, and again he sported about the guests, and was caressed and admired as before. It was an odd coincidence, that one of the Pisan ambassadors conceived such a fancy for the dog that he begged the Cardinal to bestow it upon him. The Cardinal, quite forgetting his *impromptu* gift to the noble Florentine, very courteously told the Pisan to consider the dog his own. A little later, a messenger came from the Florentine ambassador to claim the dog, and it was promptly delivered. When the Pisan ambassador's messenger arrived for the same purpose, the dog was gone. The Pisan was greatly enraged, and insisted that the dog was his by right, and should be yielded up to him. The Florentine refused to relinquish his highly valued pet. The ambassadors met in the streets of Rome, and an angry argument ensued. They did not hesitate to insult one another grossly, and furious words were followed by furious blows. A regular street fray was the sequence. The Pisans came off the victors, for the Pisan ambassadors were accompanied by fifty Pisan soldiers. All the Florentines in Rome at once assembled and attacked the Pisans, and in this second contest, the battle appears to have ended in favor of the Florentines.

When the news of this dissension reached Pisa,

the Government of that city immediately took possession of all the merchandise in Pisa which belonged to Florentine citizens. The Florentines
made every effort to have their property restored,
without extending the quarrel farther; but the
Pisans were deaf to all offers of reconciliation, and
refused to give up the goods, of which there was a
very large quantity, waiting to be imported in
Pisan ships. The patience of the Florentines became exhausted, and they marched out and gave
battle to the obstinate Pisans. The encounter
lasted the whole day — many lives were lost — the
Pisans were wholly defeated, and the Florentines
marched back with thirteen hundred prisoners,
among whom were numerous members of the first
families in Pisa. *Query* — Had the Cardinal's
pretty lap-dog never existed, or had it been less at-
tractive, or had the Cardinal been less liberally
careless in his donations, would that terrible day's
fighting ever have occurred ? Would those heaps of
dead have been left on the plains of *Castel del
Bosco*, and would those thirteen hundred prisoners
have been carried in triumph to Florence ?

In the " Florentine Feuds " we narrated the thrilling story of the handsome but inconsequent young
Buondelmonte, and the origin of the terrible *Guelph*
and *Ghibelline* feud. That protracted and bloody

strife had nominally ended, when it was succeeded by the feud between the *Bianchi* (White Party) and the *Neri* (Black Party), which, in the commencement of the fourteenth century, *grew out of the gambols of two children.*

The children were cousins. Their mothers were daughters of the same father, though by different wives. They belonged to the most wealthy and powerful family of Pistora — the *Cancelliere.* Each sister boasted of more than a hundred retainers. The name of one sister was *Bianca,* hence her descendants were called *Cancelliere Bianchi ;* the offsprings of the other sister, for distinction's sake, were called *Cancelliere Neri.* [In Italy the maiden name is always retained, and that of the husband is often made to *precede*, instead of following, the lady's family name.]

Young *Loré* the son of *Guglielmo de Cancelliere* (*Neri*), while playing with his cousin, the son of *Bertuca de Cancelliere* (*Bianchi*), accidentally inflicted a serious wound. The father of Loré was much distressed when he heard of this chance injury, and at once sent Loré to the father of the wounded boy to express his contrition, and to beg forgiveness both of father and son.

Loré's apologies and explanations were fiercely interrupted by his inhuman uncle, who cried out:

" Boy, you were not prudent in showing your face here: neither was your father wise in sending you!"

He then turned to a servant, and bade him summon the cook, and order him to bring his cleaver. When the latter appeared, his master pointed to the affrighted Loré, and then to a horse-trough near, and commanded the servants to hold the child while the cook struck off his right hand (the hand which had injured his cousin) upon the horse-trough. The cook and the servants did not dare to disobey, the child's hand was quickly severed. His uncle savagely seized the fallen member, and, placing it in the boy's other hand, said: " Take *that* to thy father from me."

The Neri, maddened by a deed so cowardly and so cruel, summoned retainers and friends, flew to arms, and attacked the *Bianchi*. The citizens joined in the fray, some taking sides with one party, some with the other. The chiefs of the two parties were exiled from Pistora, and sent to Florence. There the *Bianchi* were received by the *Cerchi*, and the *Neri* by the *Donati* and *Frescobaldi* families. The more aristocratic portion of the community sided with the *Neri*, the Guelph populace supported the *Bianchi*, and a most bloody warfare, in which all the distinguished men of that age took part, broke out, and gave birth to numberless acts of inconceivable barbarity. The great Dante upheld the *Bianchi.*

Between the *Cerchi* and *Donati* families, who had ranged themselves, the one on the side of the *Bianchi*, the other of the *Neri*, a most irreconcilable feud existed.

The *Cerchi* were very opulent merchants, the *Donati* impoverished nobles. Unfortunately they were neighbors. The *Cerchi* had purchased one of the magnificent old palaces which had belonged to the *Guidi.* Near by resided the *Donati* in a more humble mansion. The *Cerchi* made a prodigal display of their wealth; they kept many servants, horses and equipages, and the young men, awkward and plebeian, though handsome and intelligent, dressed with surpassing splendor.

Corso, the head of the *Donati* family, openly ridiculed the manners, bearing, and low-bred ostentation of his *parvenu* neighbor. He nicknamed *Vieri de Cerchi* the *donkey of the ward*, and, when *Vieri* was to speak in council, would ask "if the donkey had brayed that day?"

The historian, Dino Compagni, says of *Corso Donati :* "He was of noble race, handsome in person, a good speaker, of elegant manners, and of a subtle intelligence, *allied to a heart always intent on evil.* He and his band committed many deeds of arson and robbery in the city. On account of his arrogance he was nicknamed "*the baron.*"

Dante married Gemma, a member of this *Donati* family, and in his youth, strange to say, was much attached to the fierce, unscrupulous "Baron." In after years they became deadly foes, and *Corso Donati* was one of the most powerful instruments in promoting Dante's banishment from Florence, in procuring a decree for the confiscation of his property, and in sentencing him to be burned at the stake if he ever fell into the hands of the Florentine Government.

It was almost impossible for the members of the *Donati* and *Cerchi* families to meet without fighting.

One day they were both at the funeral of a lady of the *Frescobaldi* family. The nobles had the privilege of sitting upon benches; all others sat on reed mats. The *Cerchi* and *Donati* found themselves placed opposite to each other — the treasureless *Donati* upon their seats of honor, and the opulent *Cerchi* on the ground, almost at their feet. This position galled the one party, and rendered the other insolently exultant. They watched each other's movements with angry eyes. During the ceremony, one of the *Cerchi* rose from his seat, it is said, merely to adjust the folds of his dress beneath him. The *Donati* imagined that he had started up to commit some violence. They all rose in haste, drew their swords, and regardless of the sacred place, which was over the corpse lying before the altar, and the priest performing the funeral rites, the two parties rushed furiously upon each other, and were with difficulty separated.

In that same year (1300) they had another encounter, which ended more disastrously. On the evening of the first day of the annual May festivities, a party of ladies were dancing on the Piazza di Santa Trinita, surrounded by an admiring crowd. Among the lookers-on were a group of the young *Cerchi* and their friends, mounted on their horses. Soon the *Donati*, also mounted, joined the crowd, and pressed forward to obtain a view of the dancers. Accidentally the two parties pushed each other. In a moment swords flashed from their scabbards; the dance was broken up; the terrified ladies fled, shrieking, to their homes — the Piazza, which a moment before had echoed to gay music, now resounded with the clash of arms, the trampling of horses' hoofs, and the cries of the charging foes. Furious combatants met where the feet of fair women had so lately glided through the graceful measure; riot and confusion usurped the place of gayety and gallantry. One of the *Cerchi* had his nose cut off by a *Donati* sabre. When the fight ended, a new element of hatred, and a stronger thirst for revenge, had been infused into the minds of these adversaries.

On Christmas Day of the same year, two members of the opposing families came again into collision. A holy friar was preaching on the Piázza, in front of the Church Santa Croce. *Simone Donati* formed one of the listening crowd. *Nicola de Cerchi* came riding by alone, on his way to a villa without the city. *Simone*, at the sight of a *Cerchi* unprotected, turned from the pious exhortation of the good friar, spurred his horse, and came up with his unguarded foe outside of the city walls, attacked him unexpectedly, and murdered him on the spot! But *Niccola*, as he fell from his horse, struck at *Simone*, and inflicted a wound with his dagger, from which *Simone* died the next day.

This Simone was the son of *Messer Corso Donati*, " the Baron," who became very celebrated in Florentine history; we constantly see him at the head of the party disturbing the public peace, and committing all manner of outrages. IIis cruelty seems to have extended itself alike to men and women, as his treatment of his beautiful sister, Piccarda, illustrates. In spite of her opposition, he promised her hand to *Rossellino della Tosca*. To avoid this hateful union, she fled, during her brother's absence, to the Convent of St. Clare, and took the vows of a nun. When *Corso Donati* heard this news he hastened to Florence, assembled twelve ruffians, and with them scaled the walls of the convent, seized his sister, and, regardless of the holy vows she had made, gave her to *Rossellino della Tosca*. But she was soon rescued from a merciless brother and a pitiless husband. The horror of her situation and the terrible scenes through which she had passed, snapped the cord which bound her to a life of despair. She only survived her union a few days.

Corso Donati's end was a fitting termination to his turbulent and lawless career. In 1308, he was suspected of conspiring to become despotic master of the Commonwealth. He was declared guilty by the *Podestá*, and condemned to death. But he and his allies strongly barricaded the streets adjacent to his house, and gave battle to the party who came to seize him. While defending the barricade in front, he was attacked in the rear; but he succeeded in cutting his way through the enemy, and with a few trusty friends reached *Rovezzano*, a villa three miles from the city. There he was overtaken, disarmed, and finally captured. He was resolved not to be carried into the city alive, to be subjected to the scoffs of the rabble, and be consigned to the hands of the executioner. He tried to bribe his captors to kill him, but in vain. There was no means of self-destruction within his reach, and his bodily exertions had brought on a sudden and violent attack of gout in the feet and hands. He was now within one mile of the city, and desperate. Suddenly, he threw himself from his horse to the ground. The soldier who was guarding him imagined that he was making an attempt to escape, and pinned him to the earth with his lance. Thus Donati's stratagem succeeded, and he never more entered the walls of Florence. The soldiers left his body in the road. The monks of St. Salvi found it the next day, and buried it in their cemetery.

SERRAVEZZA.

SERRAVEZZA, Aug. 15, 1865.

IN one of the valleys of the marble district of the Apennines lies the little village of Serravezza. The rivers Serra and Vezza, threading their way between the mountains, suddenly bend and unite, and the village built upon their banks, at the point of union, takes the combined name of both rivers. The mills belonging to the marble quarries are worked by the waters of these rivers. They are narrow streams, that gracefully wind in and out, now gliding smoothly, and now leaping over rocks and forming unexpected cascades. The banks are richly wooded, and here and there the trees dip into the stream. The verdant mountains start up, almost perpendicularly, on either side, the green of their chestnut, fig, and olive trees often suddenly interrupted by "*slides*" (as they are called) of gleaming white marble.

The little village of Serravezza is quaint and primitive, but picturesque in a high degree. It is

composed of a mere cluster of houses planted together in a narrow strip along the banks of the river,
and girdled in by the mountains.   Yet it has a somewhat imposing little church, with the Duomo and
Campanile, adorned within by pictures and statues
of no small merit.   Beside the church stands a hospital, a large commodious building, endowed by
Cavaliere Campana.   The constant accidents in the
mountains and in the quarries render this admirably conducted hospital a most important institution.
Every day its doors admit some poor sufferer whose
limbs have been crushed by a fall of marble, or
who has met with some other disaster inseparable
from his vocation.

At the head of the valley, commanding a superb
prospect, stands the villa of the Medici — a favorite resort of the late Grand Duke.   Situated in this
small, secluded, peaceful-looking village, one cannot
help wondering to see this unpretending looking
villa well provided with *port holes* for cannon, as
if the attacks of an enemy were at all times anticipated.   A subterranean passage runs for a mile beneath the mountain, and leads from the villa to the
sea-shore.   Here the Medici always kept a vessel
prepared for their escape.   The villa has spacious
stables, with accommodations for thirty-six horses ;
also, a chapel, and a large garden surrounded by

massive stone walls. Close by is a marble quarry, which belonged to this noble family. The property of the Medici is now held by the Government of Victor Emmanuel. The town authorities of Serravezza express great discontent because no title-deed proves that the ground upon which the Medician villa stands has ever been paid for. Victor Emmanuel offers the villa for sale, that the authorities may receive the price they demand for the land. The villa, it is said, cost between thirty and forty thousand dollars to build — it is offered for sale for *eight thousand !*

In the centre of the village stands a stone column, out of which rises an iron spike, placed there to receive the gory head of the decapitated traitor. Doubtless, before the Tuscan law forbade capital punishment, it has often been capped by this ghastly adorning.

The little village, small and obscure as it is, boasts of its men of genius — or, rather, of *embryo* genius. It may be the close proximity to the marble, or that the vocation of stone earth is one low step in the ascent to high art, but among these stone-cutters there is a small band aspiring to become sculptors — making uncouth attempts to cut figures in stone, hideous apes, wild beasts, and other ungraceful forms ; but from among these rude essays, some beautiful creation will no doubt one day spring beneath the hand of genius yet undeveloped.

And Serravezza boasts of a musical genius — a young man of twenty years, occupied in the iron foundry, who composes and improvises music in the most wonderful manner. He is self-taught. The only instrument he could afford to purchase is an accordeon, but listening to him, as he played beneath our window the other evening, it seemed absolutely incredible that the instrument from which he was drawing such touching strains — now so strong and full, now so meltingly sweet and echoing, so delicate and varied — *could* have been a simple accordeon.

Then Serravezza has her decayed actor, once the representative of Roman Emperors and Greek Kings, but who now, in the " sere and yellow leaf " of his life, condescends to keep an *albergo*, or inn — we could hardly venture to designate the humble locality as a *hôtel*. This dramatic satellite amuses his patrons, not merely by reciting passages from celebrated plays, but often by going through whole tragedies, admirably personating each character in turn. His declamation is remarkable for its power and pathos, and though he is quite an old man, his gestures have an eloquent grace peculiar to the Italian.

The native poet, or *improvisatore*, we learn, is often to be met with here. And surely, if there is one spark of poetic fire in the breast, it must be fanned into life by the grandeur and beauty of these glorious mountains.

Albeit the scenery of the Apennines, in these regions though different in character, is as grandly beautiful as that of the finest portions of Switzerland, strange to say, the latter is flooded with tourists, while these picturesque Apennine peaks, only three hours' journey by railroad from Florence, are scarcely visited.

The Pania, the highest of the range, is reached after six hours' climbing, starting from Serravezza. From its summit the whole coast of the Mediterranean, from Spezzia to Leghorn, is visible, viâ Reggio, Leghorn, Pisa, and even Florence can be distinctly seen: the latter is sixty miles distant.

A natural bridge connects two of the mountains at their very peaks, 5000 feet above the level of the sea. This bridge is a narrow stone ledge, its arch 160 feet high. It is called the " Madonna's Bridge," and the *contadini* implicitly believe the tradition, that the Madonna, in passing over these mountains, desired to step from one mountain peak to the peak adjoining, when immediately the stone formed itself into a bridge, barely wide enough to permit her dainty feet to walk over in safety.

Some of the marble quarries are several thousand feet above the level of the river; a few of them are near the very topmost peaks of the mountains.

The marble is blasted in the mountains, then cut into square blocks, then hurled over the side of a mountain, upon a marble "*slide*," down which it makes its way with tremendous bounds, the whole mountain echoing the roar, while smaller pieces of marble, with which it comes in contact in its frantic descent, leap into the air, sometimes to the height of sixty feet, enveloped in a cloud of snow-white marble dust.

The "*slide*" of marble leads from the quarry to the valley. Across this "*slide*," at various distances, are erected walls of marble, which give the block the direction required, and cause it to fall upon the ground in the valley, upon the exact place prepared, and where it can be reached by ox carts.

Near each quarry are the marble works of the proprietors, large, handsome buildings, looking like railway stations, where all the process of sawing the marble and polishing is accomplished by water-power.

The marble is taken in ox-carts to the *Forte di Marma,* four miles from Serravezza. In calm weather, the oxen are driven, most unwillingly, into the sea to the boats. When the weather is too boisterous for them to be forced into the water, the small vessels in which the marble is to be conveyed to Leghorn are drawn upon the beach, and there loaded. The ox-carts are then fastened to the boats and the oxen (sometimes fourteen pairs at a time) urged into the sea. The marble-laden boat is thus launched.

At the *Forte di Marma* the whole beach, for a quarter of a mile, is white with blocks of marble — marble columns, pedestals, slabs, flooring — looking, at the first glance, like an endless city of monuments. At this moment are to be seen upon the beach the columns, steps, flower vases, and various decorations in colored marble, destined for the new opera house now being erected at Paris.

This beach is one of the most beautiful we have ever had the great enjoyment of walking upon. When the tide is low, the sand is smooth and firm to the foot. On one side stretches the " blue Mediterranean," far as the eye can reach; and, parallel with the shore, on the other side, rises the Apennine chain, in all its majestic beauty. And if the picturesque charm of the scene can be heightened, we have seen it brought to perfection beneath the su-

perb Italian sunset, flooding the heavens with indescribable glory, while a crowd of lovely, laughing
girls and merry children sported. upon the beach,
and dived, and danced, and gambolled in the shining water.

But to return to the marble quarries. The smaller
blocks of marble are split at the quarries into slabs,
and these slabs are carried to the beach upon the
heads of women. Some women are able to carry
four marble slabs upon their heads at a time, and
this over the roughest, steepest, and most difficult
mountain paths! This severe and unfeminine labor
earns these poor toilers for bread rarely as much
as a franc (about twenty-two cents) per day, and
never more. The habit of holding the head erect,
and poising the body as they step, causes these
women to move with a firm and graceful grandeur
of step and motion, which would throw into despair
the representatives of our stage queens (the genuine
queens are too seldom queenly in gait to be mentioned), if they could behold and then study the
regal carriage of these poor carrier peasants.

One of the favorite pastimes of the little children
is to imitate their mothers—pile cakes of mud or
stones, supposed to be marble slabs, upon their
heads, then holding themselves erect and steady,
fold their arms upon their breasts, and step from

stone to stone in the bed of the river, balancing themselves dexterously, and moving with that grand step of the mother as she descends the mountain paths.

At Serravezza there are quarries of variously colored marbles, and the scientific agriculturist may interest himself by investigating a fact which has excited the curiosity and surprise of visitors. The peculiar coloring of the different marbles appears to be repeated in the beans that grow in the valley. There is a pink marble with black veins, and there are pink beans with the same veining. There is bluish marble with spots, and there are beans to match. Greenish marble, and beans of precisely the same hue of green — by no means the ordinary green of a bean. The yellow marble has its yellow bean. There is a cream-colored marble with blue veins, and there are cream-colored beans with veins of blue. The causes which have produced these resemblances may doubtless be explained, but the singular resemblance itself cannot be explained away.

We mentioned in the early portion of this letter the villa of the Medici, which was a favorite resort of the late Grand Duke. We have only just learned, in conversing about this villa, a circumstance which does him great honor. We were not aware that he belonged to the celebrated society of the Misericordia — the Brothers of Mercy.

The members of the Misirecordia are the Good Samaritans of Tuscany, who give their own personal services to aid the suffering. Many of them belong to noble families. At the sound of the deep, sonorous summoning bell of the Duomo, however these members may be employed, whether at marriage feast, or taking rest, or occupied in the most grave and important duties of life, if it is their week to serve, they must leave all and hasten to the *Piazza del Duomo*, to present themselves at the oratory of the Misericordia. Here the brethren pass into the robing room, and issue from it, into the chapel, clothed in long black robes, with peaked hoods over their heads and faces, leaving their eyes alone visible through two holes cut in the cowl. A large, broad-leafed hat hangs at the back, over the shoulders. They form themselves into pairs, according to their height, and raising the black-covered litter prepared to receive the sufferer, walk forth with even, rapid steps, and in perfect silence. The member present who happens to be the highest in rank in the hierarchy of the Order, acts as captain, walks at the head of the procession, and directs all its movements. It is his duty to prepare the apparatus required for the last hurried shrift (should such

The " Misericordia ; " or, Secret Burial Society at Florence.—*Page* 166.

be needed) of the dying — the crucifix, the candle, the breviary, the holy oil. These are deposited in a box and attached to the litter.

The brethren are not permitted by their laws to partake of any refreshment at the house where they receive their human burden, save a glass of cold water.

They carry with them a pair of large, clean sheets and a counterpane, and with these they enter the house of the sick. The sheets are dexterously placed beneath the patient — one so as to perfectly envelop him, the other to form a sort of hammock, in which, covered with the counterpane, he is gently borne to the litter. The delicacy and care with which the brethren shield their charge from the public's curious gaze, while placing him (or her) in the litter, has often been a subject of comment. The sick person carefully deposited, the litter is raised, and the black-muffled *cortége* proceeds on its way to the hospital. It is the duty of one brother, if the sick person is supposed to be near his last moments, to keep a vigilant watch, and from time to time lift the front part of the covering. If he sees any alarming symptoms, he strikes three little blows on one of the poles. At this signal the bearers immediately set down the litter, the great black covering is thrown aside, the brethren gather round to shield the dying, as much as possible, from the gaze of the passer-by, and the sacrament is hurriedly administered.

The Grand Duke, it is said, was most punctual, earnest, and efficient in discharging all his duties as a member of this Holy Brotherhood.

THE PROTESTANT CEMETERY AT FLORENCE.

MRS. BROWNING — DR. SOUTHWOOD SMITH — MRS. FRANCES TROLLOPE, AND OTHER CELEBRITIES.

FLORENCE, Nov. —, 1865.

THERE are few localities in Florence so replete with solemn interest to the English and American traveller as the Protestant Cemetery. It is situated a short distance beyond the *Porta a Pinti*. The ground rises in gentle undulations from the entrance gate to an eminence which commands a prospect of varied and picturesque loveliness, — a gradual ascent, which seems to typify those upward steps which the spirit takes after it has thrown off the mortal clog interred in that earth.

There are not many imposing, or even pretentious monuments. The one which first attracts the eye is that of Routh Fairleigh, surmounted by a statue of Faith, by Fantachiotti.

This cemetery holds the ashes of not a few who have won renown in Great Britain and America, but the one about whose odorous memory there clings the deepest, tenderest, most widely-spread interest, is Elizabeth Barrett Browning.

She loved Italy with a deep, passionate, prayerful love and longing for its resurrection from the grave of sloth and inertia — with a prophetic foreseeing of its restored liberty and glory. Florence was so entirely the home of her heart, that she seems to belong to Italy rather than to England. In Florence the very air is redolent of her presence: go where you will, you trace her footsteps — from the heights of beautiful *Bellosguardo*, lovely *Fiesole*, or solemnly grand *San Miniato*, down to the banks of the *Arno ;* through the narrow palace-lined and legend-consecrated streets, on the gay *Cascine*, in the memorable squares, on the picturesque old bridges, in the churches, in the galleries, standing in rapt admiration before the works of old masters — everywhere the rhythmic echo of her inspired words ring in the ears. She has sung of them all, has linked herself to all by her glorious verse.

Most readers are familiar with her poem entitled "Casa Guidi Windows " — that *Casa Guidi* which now bears a tablet with the inscription —

"Here lived and died Elizabeth Barrett Browning, who united in her heart the knowledge of the Learned and the genius of the Poet, and with her verses made a golden link between Italy and England. Grateful Florence offers her this memorial, 1861."

In *Casa Guidi* her son—the only babe which ever rejoiced her yearning heart, and rendered perfect her womanhood—first drew breath. In *Casa Guidi* she said to him:

> "The sun strikes, through the windows, up the floor;
>   Out on it, my own young Florentine;
>   Not two years old, and let me see thee more!
>   It grows along thy amber curls, to shine
>   Brighter than elsewhere. Now, look straight before,
>   And fix thy brave, blue, English eyes on mine,
>   And from thy soul, which fronts the future so,
>   With unabashed and unabated gaze,
>   Teach me to hope for what the angels know,
>   When they smile clear as thou dost!
>
>   .   .   .   .
>
>   Stand out, my blue-eyed prophet!—thou to whom
>   The earliest world daylight that ever flowed
>   Through *Casa Guidi* windows chanced to come!"

In *Casa Guidi* her cold lips for the last time pressed those of her "blue eyed-prophet." From *Casa Guidi* her holy spirit took its heavenward flight, before the sorrowing watchers knew that there was one angel less on earth. It is related that in answer to the inquiry how she felt, she murmured her last words, and they were "*so lovely!*" A fitting utterance to fall from those dying lips—and how suggestive of her life! Her eyes were ever fixed upon the beautiful; or they beautified, through their own hallowing medium, what they had looked upon. It is said we are most apt to recognize in others what exists in ourselves; and hence sprang her quick recognition of all that is lovely, noble, and good. The evil that glared before eyes less merciful was ignored by hers; her spirit, wherever it moved, threw a halo of luminous holiness and beauty around even commonplace objects and natures, and lifted them up out of their dull insignificance, and converted the prosaic round of daily life into poetry.

Thousands of feet have visited her grave; thousands of hands have plucked the ivy leaves from the sod, yet uncovered by the elaborate monument which is being sculptured to adorn the spot.

The Italians, even those who are well educated, take but little interest in English literature. We think it is not too much to say they are better acquainted with Mrs. Browning's writings than with those of any other English author.

A few steps onward, past the grave of Mrs. Browning, we come to that of the celebrated Dr. Southwood Smith, a man whom England reveres as largely the benefactor of his race. His monument, of pure white Serravezza marble, bears this inscription, from the pen of Leigh Hunt:

"Ages shall honor, in their heart enshrined thee,
SOUTHWOOD SMITH, physician of mankind, bringer
of air, light, health, in the homes of the sick poor,
of happier years to come."

A bas-relief, beautifully executed by the American sculptor, Mr. Hart, calls vividly to mind the features of the philanthropist — features almost perfect in their benign and holy beauty. The ample brow, the finely shaped eyes, the exquisitely soft and benignant mouth, the whole contour of the face, manifest the soul of the man as few souls reveal themselves through their covering of clay.

Mr. Hart has invented an ingenious instrument, which enables him to repeat, by exact measurement, the features of his sitter. He used this instrument in sculpturing the bas-relief of Dr. Southwood Smith. Thus there can be no question of the correctness of the proportions and the faithfulness of the likeness. We are aware that Mr. Hart's invention has been ridiculed by some of his brother artists, who prefer to exercise their powers of idealizing upon a portrait, and to improve upon defective nature; but the public, who desire to know precisely how a great man looked, is Mr. Hart's debtor. We learn that, of late, some of the best artists in Florence have not disdained, now and then, to ask permission to use this " mechanical invention," to test the exactness of their own delineations.

The life of Dr. Southwood Smith is rich in incident. One of the most touching is that to which his noble work on the Divine Government and his valuable and instructive volume on the Physiology of Health owe their origin.

Very early in life he became a Calvinist clergyman. One beautiful Saturday afternoon he was passing through a field in a little village where he had just arrived, and where he was to preach on the morrow. Suddenly he heard behind him the sound of musical voices, and of merry laughter. He turned and saw five young girls. A moment after they passed him, still laughing and talking. With the face of one he was powerfully impressed, and her voice thrilled him as though it had been a loved and familiar tone. It may seem strangely romantic to the wide range of commonplace people, but the young clergyman, who was only nineteen years of age, watched the merry maidens until they reached a stile and climbed over. The young girl who had so singularly attracted him came last, and when she had stepped over and gone on her way, the already enamored boy rushed to the spot, and kneeling down, kissed the ground which he had seen pressed by her feet. The lovely face and melodious voice haunted him all that night. The next morning, when he entered the pulpit, his eyes fell upon the same countenance looking up to his. The five young ladies, with an elderly gentleman, were sitting directly before him.

When the service concluded, several of the parishioners were presented, and among them the father of the five sisters. This gentleman invited the young clergyman to his house. From that hour an intimacy commenced, which resulted in Southwood Smith's winning the heart of the fair girl whom he had literally loved at the first glance. Before the close of the year the father died, leaving his five motherless daughters to the guardianship of the youthful clergyman.

Southwood Smith was only twenty when he became a bridegroom, and, although his bride was a few years his senior, their union is said to have been one of unmitigated happiness. In less than four years he was the father of two daughters — and they were motherless. When her last infant was only a few months old, his wife took a severe cold, while visiting the poor, and, after a brief illness, expired.

The grief of the widower amounted to despair — almost to frenzy. For a season he could find no consolation ; but, pondering upon the decrees of that

Divine Providence which could permit such a calamity, the light of truth pierced through the clouds of rebellion that enveloped his mind, and he wrote his eloquent book upon the Divine Government — truly the healing offspring of his wounded spirit. He, however, entertained the conviction that his wife might have been spared to him, had she not been unskilfully and ignorantly treated ; and he was so impressed with this idea, that, in the compassionate hope of saving others from needlessly enduring the terrible blow which had crushed his life, he left the ministry and studied medicine. This erudite and instructive work upon the Physiology of Health was the result of his laborious investigations and deductions.

He not only became an eminent physician, but to him England is indebted for her sanitary improvements, and to him the science of medicine owes much of its progress, and the revelation of various facts until then unsuspected.

The last year of his life was passed in Florence, the home of his youngest daughter.

In another part of the cemetery is the grave of the celebrated Mrs. Frances Trollope, the mother of the distinguished authors, Anthony Trollope and T. Adolphus Trollope. Mrs. Trollope's name is familiar to all Americans, and it has been difficult for them to pardon her first literary effort — a volume in which she so savagely, and with such one-sided pertinacity ridiculed their foibles and peculiarities, without doing justice to what is grand and noble in the national character. But her experiences in America were confined to a very limited sphere — chiefly Western — and no one can read her book without perceiving how little opportunity she had of judging Americans out of that narrow circle.

Mrs. Trollope had reached her fortieth year before she aspired to become an authoress; but her pen proved wonderfully fruitful, and her numerous works of fiction won her not merely fame, but fortune.

We remember her well in Paris, when her drawing-room was the centre of attraction to artists and men of letters. She was a vivacious, agreeable, and amiable lady, who possessed the enviable talent not merely of shining herself, but of making others shine. It was her delight to stretch out a helping hand to struggling talent. She was never weary of encouraging the faint-hearted, and of giving the full meed of appreciation to modest worth.

During the latter portion of her life she made her home in Florence. Her mental powers had been so largely and incessantly taxed, that they gave way beneath the strain, and for some years before her death she entirely lost her memory — not precisely her reason — but certainly her intelligence. She resided at the time of her death with her son, T. Adolphus Trollope. In spite of her deplorable condition, she was far from unhappy. She always fancied herself surrounded by books, even when there was not a volume within reach, and when asked if she needed anything, replied, " No. You see I have plenty of books. I can always amuse myself." She died at an advanced age, in 1864.

Not far from her grave is that of the wife of T. Adolphus Trollope, Theodosia Trollope, who died in 1865. She also was a successful writer, and was endowed with a richly cultivated mind, great fascination of manner, charms of person, and remarkable musical talent, doubtless inherited from her mother, Madame Garrow, a prima donna well known to fame.

In accordance with the Florentine custom, the municipality has decided to place a tablet upon her residence, commemorative of her genius.

On the other side of the cemetery is the grave of Theodore Parker, well beloved on both sides of the ocean.

Recently another distinguished American name is added to those inscribed upon the tombstones of this Florentine cemetery — that of Hildreth, the historian, and author of the " White Slave." He died in Florence in 1865. Mental labors, too long protracted, occasioned softening of the brain, and reduced him to a state of childish dependence. He left a wife to fight life's hard battle single-handed, and in the field of art; also a son of promising talents, who looks forward to making a name in his own land as an architect and landscape gardener.

But our article would extend itself to a volume if we made even passing mention of all the illustrious dead whose ashes repose in this beautiful cemetery, and of whose lives a record full of interest might be given.

OVERFLOW OF THE ARNO — ARTIST, AND THE MAD SINGER.

FLORENCE, July, 1865.

IN another article we make a brief allusion to the last occasion in which Piccolomini was conjured out of her retirement, to delight the ears of Florence, and aid the sufferers from the inundation.

It was in November, 1864, that the capricious little Arno, which is always playing "fantastic tricks before high Heaven," spread dismay through the startled city, by one of its maddest pranks.

The beauty of this slender stream, which pierces the heart of Florence, has been sung by poets and lauded by travellers. Mrs. Browning, as she views it from the lovely heights of Bellosguardo, speaks of —

" The river trailing like a silver cord."

Again, looking from her Casa Guidi windows, she says :

> "I can but muse in hope upon the shore
> Of *golden Arno* as it shoots away
> Thro' Florence's heart, beneath her bridges four:
> Bent bridges, seeming to strain off like bows,
> And tremble while the arrowing undertide
> Shoots on and cleaves the marble as it goes,
> And strikes up palace walls on either side."

Byron, too, speaks of the " Arno's *silver* sheen."

We have seen the Arno justify the poetic simile of a " *silver cord,*" when its waters were clear, and the full moon seemed melted in the gently flowing stream ; and we have seen the chameleon-like Arno look like a "golden cord " in the noonday sun, or when it reflected the countless lights flashing along its banks during the city's illumination for some grand *festa ;* and we have often seen this same changeful Arno degraded into a narrow, reddish, and decidedly muddy current, the very opposite of "*silver,*" "*golden,*" or "*picturesque ;* " and not unfrequently we have beheld its waters almost entirely vanish, and bright-eyed Italian *gamins* gambol in its shallow bed.

Twice within three years the Arno has suddenly swelled and overflowed its banks. The last inundation, that of November, 1864, was the most serious that has occurred during the last twenty years.

The little circle, of which we formed a part, was residing at the time in the *Via Dei Bardi* — a street which Miss Evans has rendered famous by making it the home of her noble Romola. We chanced to be located very near where Romola is supposed to have lived, and within view of the hill where Tessa tended her hidden babes and watched for her false-hearted Tito. This *Via Dei Bardi* was one of the streets metamorphosed into a river by the inundation.

It was on a quiet Sunday morning that we were startled by the tidings that the river had suddenly risen, and was overflowing its banks. An artist friend, who had crossed the nearest bridge an hour before, without anticipating any danger, was paying us a visit. He started up in dismay, fearing that he might be cut off from his home, seized his hat, and hastily departed. We could well imagine there was some cause for his alarm when we saw him carried across the garden upon the back of a man who waded knee-deep through the water.

Half an hour after, in rushed another friend, who had seen, from his villa on the *Bellosguardo* heights, the swollen river and our perilous situation should the overflow be serious. He came with characteristic hospitality to urge us to take flight to his Bellosguardo home before we became prisoners. We could none believe that the tiny, harmless looking stream which we were accustomed to regard as a " *silver*," or " *golden*," or muddy " *cord*," could work any decided mischief, and refused the kind offer. Our friend hurried away, and, as we watched his departure, we found that the water had risen too high for him to be borne out upon a man's back. He was compelled to call in the assistance of a donkey, and made his way through the garden, seated in a rude *barroccio*, drawn by a donkey, whose legs were completely hidden by the reddish current.

Our situation began to look a little threatening. The wisdom of following the undignified example of our friend, and making our escape seated on the floor of a furniture wagon, and dragged by an ignoble donkey, was discussed. We concluded to wait a few hours longer. Before the time appointed for our final decision arrived, the power to choose was taken from us.

The kitchen and billiard room were under water; the *concierge* had locked the massive entrance portals of the palace, and fled; the water had risen above their bolts and locks, above the windows of the *piano terrena* (ground floor) and was approaching those of the *entresol*. We had watched it ascend the whole first flight of stairs leading to our apartments, and it had gained the first step of the last flight. The street had been suddenly transformed into a river. Boats, sent by the authorities for the relief of the poor, were passing rapidly up and down; articles of furniture, beds, women and children, were being lifted out of the windows of the lower stories and carried away.

As for us, the windows of our *entresol* were strongly grated, and those of the apartments we occupied, on the floor above, were too distant from the boats for escape to be possible; we were literally water-bound prisoners.

Soon came a report that the authorities feared the parapets of the river would give way; the destruction must then be terrible, incalculable, many houses must inevitably be swept away, and numerous lives sacrificed. The excitement throughout the streets in peril may be better conceived than described. Though the month was November, every window was open, the whole length of the *Via Dei Bardi,* and pale, anxious faces, peered out, watching the rising of the water; and now and then a frightened voice cried to the *gens d'armes* in the boats, and in piteous tones asked how great was the danger.

Thus passed the day. About midnight the waters ceased to rise. During the night, to our inexpressible relief, they gradually subsided. The next day, however, boats still made their way along many of the flooded streets.

As may be imagined, the losses and sufferings of
of the poor were very great. Florence displayed a
charitable munificence, and contributions for their
aid flowed in almost as rapidly and abundantly as
the waters of the Arno when they caused the calamity. Charity, according to her custom in the present day, assumed the pleasant form of public enter-
tainments, as a lure. At some of these, " stars that
had set " rose again; among them Piccolomini
shone forth with undiminished radiance.

We were residing, at the time of the inundation
in the Palazzo Sabatier — the home of Madame
Ungker Sabatier, one of the greatest celebrities in
Florence, the distinguished German *prima donna*,
the contemporary and rival of Malibran.

This palace was built in 1400, and belonged at
one time to the Bonaparte family. It was the residence of the present Emperor Napoleon Bonaparte.
It passed from the hands of the Bonapartes into
those of the Alamanni, thence to the Pitti family,
and from the latter was purchased by Monsieur
Sabatier.

The principal drawing-room of this palace is
certainly one of the most remarkable *salons* in Florence. Its decorations are singularly beautiful and
original. The entire wall is covered with a canvas
overlaid with gold. Upon this golden ground life-

sized pictures have been skilfully painted by the eminent French artists Bonquet and Papety.

On one side we have Shakespeare — Shakespeare in his youth, by Papety ; beyond, Mozart standing before his piano ; and further on, Don Giovanni, with the fair deluded ones, and the ghost in the background.   These paintings were all executed by Papety.

Next we see Dante, led by the spirit of Virgil, and above, *Francesca di Rimini* borne to heaven. This group is by Bonquet.

Farther on, we behold Raphael, standing between Mephistopheles and Faust, who is embracing Margaret.

Then comes Raphael, leaning against an easel which holds the unfinished picture of the *Madonna della Seggiola ;* above, a half-nude female figure, either representing Fame or *La Fornarina*, holds a crown over the head of Raphael.   One cannot help being struck by the *posé* of Raphael, which is singularly *French ;* and even his face, though the resemblance to his portrait has been preserved, is *Frenchified* in a wonderful manner.

Next appears Michael Angelo, standing between two of his most celebrated statues, conspicuous for their muscular development.

Molière, unfinished, completes the distinguished

assemblage. The four last-mentioned groups are by Bonquet, who died while he was painting the Moliere. It is a singular coincidence, that Papety also died before his work was completed.

Bonquet left a young daughter, who has been lovingly adopted by Madame Sabatier, an enthusiastic admirer of genius. This gifted girl, at an early age, testified that the rich inheritance of her father's talents had descended to her. She has now become a highly accomplished artiste, and is at this moment completing a painting which will fill the one space on the golden ground left vacant by her father's death. Thus the hand of the daughter replaces, and it is said most ably, the death-stricken hand of the father.

The mantelpiece of this artistic drawing room is particularly worthy of mention. It may better be called a monument to Fourier than a mantelpiece — a monument of white marble, executed by the French sculptor *Ottin*. A bust of the great philanthropist Fourier looks down upon *basso riliéve* illustrative of his peculiar views, explained by inscriptions in golden letters. On either side, beneath the mantel-shelf, a couple of lovely children, life size, delight the eyes with their innocent and eloquent beauty.

M. Sabatier is a St. Simonian and a Fourierist —

an erudite scholar, an able writer, a painter of acknowledged talent, and a most eloquent conversationalist.

Madame Sabátier retired from her profession some twenty years ago. An undying passion for her glorious art daily evinces itself in her quick appreciation of youthful talent, and her lavish generosity in its cultivation. She devotes the larger portion of her time to training pupils *gratis*, for the opera or concert room — especially pupils whose limited means would have forbidden the culture of their gifts, save for her unmeasured liberality. When she has the good fortune to be thrown into contact with genius of a high order, her exertions to promote its development have no bounds; she will take the pupil to her own home, treat her as a daughter, train her with unwearied patience, scarcely eat, scarcely sleep, because of her great delight in her work of love. And when she has fitted the neophyte to encounter her public ordeal, the loving hands of the noble instructress spare no pains in smoothing the rough paths which even the most successful artist must tread, and in plucking away the thorns which ever grow among the roses with which the world crowns its favorites.

Several of Madame Sabátier's pupils have

achieved great triumphs, and hold positions of *prime donne* of the first rank.

This generous, large-hearted, highly cultivated artiste, at sixty, is full of enthusiasm, vigor, animation, and energy, and retains much of the freshness and buoyancy of her youth. She has not the faintest comprehension of that vanity which tempts women of lesser renown to conceal their ages. The year of her birth is inscribed beneath her portrait. That of her husband is written beneath his, though he is twenty years her junior. In spite of this disparity their tastes are so well adapted, their minds so thoroughly congenial, and their lives so full of active goodness, that their union seems to have been one of rare felicity.

The subject of musicians calls to mind a very singular instance of natural musical capacity that has recently awakened our interest. Tobia Sernesi was a *granatajo*, or vender of berries, about the streets of Florence. His superb voice attracted the attention of some lovers of music, who, after having afforded him a rather hurried and impromptu preparation, procured his appearance, in opera, at one of the minor theatres in Florence. In spite of his lack of culture and musical skill, his voice, a pure *baritone*, was so magnificent, that he became very popular, and after a few seasons was engaged at the

Pagliano. For some time he has completely lost his mind. We have never been able to learn to what cause his mental derangement is attributed. He may often be seen wandering about the streets, fantastically dressed, in Zouave trousers and jacket, with a red fez upon his head, singing snatches of opera music, looking wildly about him, and making the most extraordinary gesticulations. His sad-looking wife invariably follows him, at a short distance, always keeping him in sight, and hastening to the rescue whenever he gets into any difficulty.

Strange to say, when he enters the theatre he becomes perfectly reasonable — that is, in regard to all that concerns his vocation. He goes through rehearsals with precision, enacts his *rôle* at night respectably (his talents as an actor are not remarkable), sings the music correctly, and makes the proper entrances and exits without betraying any eccentricity. He is even capable of studying new characters, and of personating them, quite as well as before his misfortune; and yet out of the theatre he is absolutely *insane.*

Here is a singular study open to the psychologist — one which we hope will attract attention and receive investigation.

FEDI THE SCULPTOR.

FLORENCE, July, 1865.

"HAVE you seen Fedi's group?" is one of the
first questions the lover of art asks of a stranger now
visiting Florence. Fedi's group is the new marvel of
this beautiful city. Indeed, Fedi himself excites in
us no measured amount of wonder. He presents the
rare instance of a man who springs suddenly, with
one gigantic bound, from absolute obscurity to the
topmost round of the ladder of fame.

A few years ago Pio Fedi, the Florentine sculptor,
was comparatively unknown. He had conceived,
studied, and worked — had executed numerous statues, but none of them compelled recognition by the
unmistakable impress of genius.

Fedi commenced life as an engraver. A disease
of the eyes rendered it necessary for him to abandon
this profession. He had reached his twenty-fourth
year before he first took clay in his uncertain hands,
and received his delightful conviction that the powers

of the sculptor lay dormant within his soul. Earnest, yet unexpansive in his nature; quiet, even shrinking in his manners, he worked almost in seclusion, unaided, unregarded.

The conception of his group, representing the *enlèvement* of Polyxena by Pyrrhus, appears to have been an inspiration as sudden as it was genuine. Fedi shut himself in his studio and toiled incessantly to create in clay the superb ideal that existed within his mind. Models, and the best that could be found, were indispensable. He was poor, and to hoard up his narrow means that he might obtain these models he was often forced to deprive himself of the necessaries of life — sometimes his only food was bread and cheese and salads; but no privation which the prosecution of his work demanded was too severe. At the end of fourteen months the clay was completed. Pyrrhus has slain Polites, one of the sons of Hecuba, and bears away her youngest daughter, Polyxena, to immolate her upon the tomb of Achilles.

The majestic masterpiece won almost instantaneous recognition from the ablest judges. Crowds flocked to the studio, whose doors until then had so seldom unclosed to admit the stranger. Some raved about the grandeur of the conception, some were enchanted with the finished beauty of the execution, some were amazed at the wonderful anatomy; but all united in declaring that the entire group was a sublime triumph of art.

So grand a work must at once be perpetuated in marble; that was the public verdict. A committee was formed to raise a subscription for the purchase of the marble and the payment of workmen. Prince Ferdinand Strozzi was the president of this committee, and Peruzzi its secretary. Thirteen thousand dollars was the sum required. Only eleven thousand were raised and Fedi himself subscribed the two remaining thousands.

The cost of a pedestal was furnished by the municipality.

Thus the gifted artist, far from profiting by his work, was compelled to advance a large sum from his own slender means to ensure its execution in marble.

Our readers are doubtless aware that the sculptor moulds his design in clay, and there his labor ordinarily ends. After the clay has been cast in plaster, skilful workmen chisel the marble by measurement, and it is seldom touched by the sculptor. But Fedi worked constantly upon the marble himself, leading his workmen, and finishing all the delicate details. He was in love with his glorious creation, and experienced the most enthusiastic delight in beholding, and feeling it grow beneath his own hands.

At the expiration of eight years the stupendous group stood in marble.

It has been beautifully said, that *clay* is the *birth*, *plaster* the *death*, and *marble* the *resurrection* of sculpture. No one can watch the three phases through which a statue passes, without being forcibly struck by the truth of the comparison. The design in clay gives us a strong sense of its intrinsic beauty and expression; we see it in plaster and it looks dull, prosaic, lifeless; but in marble it re-awakens into higher, more imposing, more spiritual beauty.

The committee which Prince Strozzi headed stipulated that Fedi should not repeat his group, in order that Florence might be assured the sole honor of its possession.

The Duke of Manchester offered to purchase it from the sculptor for five thousand pounds sterling, but his offer was declined.

An ex-mayor of New York, recently visited Fedi's studio, and was so much struck by the magnificence of the colossal group, that he offered twenty-five thousand dollars to have it repeated, to adorn the New York Central Park.

Only a few days later, a most enterprising gentleman from Boston, on beholding the group, offered to pay Fedi fifty thousand dollars if he would repeat it for this same Central Park. Our Boston friend proposed to build a pavilion over the group in the Park, and charge a small price for admission, which would soon repay the original cost.

Fedi's calm, pleasant face glowed with gratification when the last munificent offer was communicated to him, and he said with animation, "I will make an appeal to the Committee, and see if it will grant me permission — it may — I cannot tell." We urged him to make the appeal without delay, and if it be not rejected, America will be enriched by a work of art which Florentine judges have pronounced the most superb of modern times.

The subject of the group is taken both from the Æneid of Virgil and the Hecuba of Euripides. The sculptor has concentrated into one separate actions of the poem and drama.

This is the story: Achilles having slain Troilus, one of the beloved sons of Priam and Hecuba, the mother becomes frantic with grief, and determines to revenge herself by means of stratagem. She makes known to Paris that Achilles has solicited the hand of her daughter Polyxena, and that they are to be united in the temple of Apollo, and plans with Paris the capture and death of the invincible hero. Paris chooses the bravest of his Phrygian soldiers, and consults with them in the temple. When Achilles enters to receive the hand of

Polyxena, they rush forth, surround, and slay him. As soon as Troy was taken, Pyrrhus, the son of Achilles, entered the palace of Priam, to take vengeance upon the murderer of his father. He slew Polites in the presence of his parents, and completed the sacrifice by killing Priam upon the dead body of his son. Thus says Virgil.

The tradition further declares that Pyrrhus, after slaying Priam and Polites, immolated upon the tomb of Achilles the beautiful Polyxena, innocent cause of the great hero's death.

The sculptor has supposed that the seizure of Polyxena took place immediately after the murder of her father and brother. Thus the *situation* (if we may use a theatrical expression) is stronger and more thrilling than described by Virgil or Euripides.

The action of the different figures composing the group conveys the idea that Polyxena has been defended by Polites and by Hecuba, and that Pyrrhus has snatched her first from the hands of her brother and then from those of her mother. Polites lies at the feet of Pyrrhus in death agony, yet vainly endeavoring to rise. Hecuba kneels, almost prostrate, with her arms lifted despairingly towards her child, as though making a last frantic effort to save her. The delicate, maidenly form of the terrified Polyxena is encircled by the strong arms of the inexorable Pyrrhus, who is bearing her off to the sacrifice.

Luigi Delatre, in his pamphlet upon the most desirable locality for the group, says, " the style of Fedi is one entirely new to us, and does not resemble the somewhat material style of Giambologna, nor the conventional style of Canova, nor the rather hard style of Bartolini, but proceeds directly from the study of the works of Phidias, and is the immediate fruit of the progress we have recently made in the recognition of the early Greek statues. This group is the first evidence of a new era in sculpture, and as such will form an epoch in the history of art."

The exact locality which the group is destined to adorn has not yet been decided. Facing the Palazzo Vecchio are three noble arcades, tastefully decorated. They were erected by Orcagna, in 1375. At one period they served for the town hall or exchange ; now they shelter an imposing assemblage of celebrated statues. It is the earnest desire of Fedi that his group should be admitted to one of these arcades — the Loggia dei Lanzi. The choice of this conspicuous and most desirable situation has excited the jealousy, and we may add the decided opposition, of other Florentine sculptors.

If this felicitous locality, enriched by the works of the most distinguished ancient and modern sculptors, *should* be selected, Fedi's group will be seen in company with works thoroughly in harmony. Ajax dying recalls Homer's Iliad. Hercules and Nestor bring to mind the "Furies" of Sophocles, even as the rape of Polyxena recalls the Æneid of Virgil and the Hecuba of Euripides. Near, we have the rape of the Sabines, by John of Bologna; the world-renowned Perseus, of Cellini; Judith slaying Holofernes, by Donatelli, etc., etc.

The Piazza Grand Duca, or Piazza della Signoria, upon which these arcades stand, is an open air museum of art. One of the most striking statues by which it is adorned is the equestrian statue of Cosimo I. by John of Bologna. Near the palace is the fountain of Neptune, by Ammanato — a colossal Neptune in a car drawn by horses, with nymphs, satyrs, and tritons sporting around. On one side of the palace is Hercules slaying Cacus, by Banchinelli; on the other, the celebrated colossal figure of David, by Michael Angelo.

To return to the group of Fedi. It was stipulated in his contract with the committee that his group should be cut out of one entire block of white marble, and that the marble should be brought either from Carrara or Serravezza. The block has proved wonderfully free from all imperfection — a fact which cannot be ascertained until after the work of chiselling has made considerable progress. The marble was brought from Carrara.

Carrara and Serravezza are the two principal villages of the Apennines.

I have already given a description of this most intetesting, picturesque, as well as quaint little village — Serravezza.

ADELAIDE RISTORI, AND PICCO-LOMINI.

Among the many celebrities who have made their homes in Florence is the renowned Italian actress, Adelaide Ristori, Marchioness del Grillo. The golden harvest reaped by her genius has reared, upon the picturesque banks of the Arno, close to the beautiful Cascine, one of the most magnificent of modern palaces. It is built of brown stone, and bears her name. The interior is lavishly decorated with superb frescoes by Agnani, who holds a prominent rank among Italian painters. The subjects represented are scenes from celebrated plays — several from Shakespeare. She has erected another palace in Paris.

Ristori has thrown double lustre upon the stage, by her resplendent talents and the shining example of her pure life. Ennobled by marriage, though less than by nature, she moves among Italy's nobility, a proud matron, reverenced by her husband and children, and worshipped by the crowd.

Her striking beauty needs no heightening at the hands of art; it is as remarkable in the drawing-room as upon the stage. Her figure is imposing; her eyes are large, and brilliantly dark; her hair is abundant, and of Oriental blackness; her brow is queenly; her mouth flexible and expressive. Her bearing is chacacterized by native grace and dignity, and, perhaps, by a slight touch of *hauteur.*

Though she has amassed a large fortune, we learn that she does not propose abandoning her profession, and converting the laurels she has not ceased to gather, during twenty-five or thirty years, into a couch of repose.

Her last performance in Florence took place on the 12th of May, 1865, the evening before the great Dante Sex-centenary Festival. Rossi and Salvini, the most eminent of Italian actors, the *Italian representatives of Shakespeare*, were compelled, by the imperative demands of the public, to interrupt their engagements in Naples and Milan, to meet Ristori in Florence. For the first time, the three brilliant luminaries shone upon the same stage. The play selected was Silvio Pellico's tragedy of Francesca da Rimini. The performance took place at the Nicolini Theatre, and elicited boundless enthusiasm.

Ristori perilled her popularity in Italy, when she acted in French to gratify a Parisian audience. It is said that the Italians openly avowed their jealous disapproval. We had the gratification of seeing her personate her first *rôle* in the French language—that of "Beatrix" in "The Madonna of Art," written expressly for her by Messrs. "*Scribe and Segouve.*" The rendition was full of pathos and grandeur, full of archness, fascination, and reality. The heroine is an actress, a *Madonna* of purity, who sacrifices all the selfish impulses of her loving heart to the glory of her profession. It is said that the authors purposely depicted Ristori's own character. Her success was triumphant. What command of the French language she has obtained, may be judged from the fact that her hypercritical, and by no means indulgent, Parisian audience applauded her to the echo, and even found a charm in the slight accent which she had not wholly conquered.

The illusion of her acting has since been in some measure destroyed to us personally, by our learning that she belongs to a school of art which we were never able to comprehend. We were told that it is not necessary for her to *feel* in order to personate *feelingly ;* it is not necessary that her own heart and eyes should be full, for her to wring the hearts, and draw tears from the eyes of others. It is said that sometimes after the grandest, most thrilling bursts of pathos, when sobs resounded on every side, and tears had been conjured into the eyes, even of the undemonstrative, Ristori, while her face was concealed from the audience, has found great diversion in exciting the merriment of some friend at the side scenes, by the most irresistibly comic looks and gestures. If this be true, and we prefer to give it the benefit of a doubt, it proves that the gifted actress' heart may be in her *art*, and not be in her *rôle*.

Another highly distinguished artist, who has lent an additional charm to Florence, by making the "City of Flowers" her home, is Piccolomini, Marchioness of Gaetani. We had last seen her smiling a witching farewell (which had almost the *sweetness* of a *closer adieu*) at the Academy of Music in New York; but her face was not less lively, her manners were not less captivating when our acquaintance was renewed in Florence in the autumn of 1864, at her palace in the street "of the angels," (*via degli angli*); an appropriate name to designate the locality of a songstress.

She had been married four years, and three cherub faces gave brightness to the room.

9*

The life of an artist has ever a touch of romance; but Piccolomini's history is enriched by a more than ordinary mingling of the romantic element.

She belongs to an ancient and noble Italian family — a family which boasts of having had a Pope and a Cardinal among its representatives. The branch from which our artist Piccolomini sprang chanced to be very restricted in its worldly possessions — not at all an uncommon circumstance among the Italian nobility. Piccolomini evinced a passion for music and the drama in her very babyhood. She was still a child when she conceived the project of studying seriously for the opera, that she might at once redeem the fortunes of her family, and enjoy the exercise of her gifts. She met with the amount of opposition from her proud relatives and aristocratic friends which was to be anticipated; but the force of that opposition had just as little power as might have been expected, when brought to bear upon the promptings of true genius. At sixteen, she made her *début* at Sienna, where her family resided. Her success was decided, though she could hardly have been called brilliant. She studied with zeal and enthusiasm, and made rapid progress in the knowledge of her art.

Musicians have never been willing to award her a high rank as a vocalist. Her voice has no great compass and no startling power, but we find compensation for what it lacks, in its varied and wonderful expression, in its melting sweetness, its ringing mirth, its sympathetic magnetism. She sings with her eyes, she sings with her eloquent hands; her whole frame is fermented with the spirit of song, and quivers, heightens, or bends, responsive to the melody that gushes from her lips. She literally and marvellously illustrates the words of the poet:

"Oh, to see or hear her singing! scarce I know which is divinest,
  For her looks sing, too; she modulates her gestures on the tune,
And her mouth stirs with the song-like song; and when the notes are finest,
  'Tis her eyes that shoot out vocal light, and seem to swell them on."

But if musical critics will not admit that her singing is "great," no one can deny that her acting is of a superlative order.

During an engagement which.she was fulfilling at Rome, an incident occurred which gave coloring to the rest of her life. One evening her attention was involuntarily attracted to a young gentleman, who always sat close to the stage, apparently absorbed in the performance. Night after night he occupied the same seat; he sat motionless, entranced, as one in a dream — never addressing any one near him, never glancing at the audience, never moving his eyes from the face of Piccolomini. And night after night, when she entered upon the scene, her eyes unconsciously turned to see if that well-known seat was filled — and filled by *him*. Soon she forgot the audience; she thought but of him, sang only *to him*. She had not the remotest idea who he was; she had no definite presentiment that they would ever meet; but he was her *inspiration*, he was her *public* — there was no other public for her when he was present.

Some weeks later, while she was paying a morning visit to a noble lady, a young gentleman entered the room, whom Piccolomini at once recognized. The lady presented her nephew. The confusion and more than wonted timidity of the youthful vocalist were inexplicable.

After this, Piccolomini and the young Marquis di Gaetani often met in society. She quickly became aware that she had given him her heart unasked. Her native pride and her maidenly delicacy rendered her so fearful that he might divine her preference — a preference which he had never solicited — that she treated him with marked coldness. He, meantime, worshipped the glorious star at a distance, never daring to dream that its light could be shed on him apart from the crowd. Though he lived but in her presence, though he hung upon her words, though he followed her from city to city, he cherished no hope that he could ever rob the public of this idol and call it his own, and his lips remained sealed.

Years passed on, and Piccolomini received and refused the most brilliant offers of marriage, and even her intimate friends imagined that her heart was untouched. She was in love with her art, they thought; there was no room in her soul for any other passion.

She appeared in London, and achieved a triumph that far surpassed all former successes. In America, also, she created a genuine *furore.* Wherever she travelled she was accompanied by her family — her father, mother, sister, and brother surrounded her, and they knew that the foot of a favored lover never entered the magic circle.

During her visit to America she accidentally learned that the young Marquis was about to be married. The shock of this intelligence was so severe, so violent, that it broke the ice beneath which she had hidden her great love, and, in her anguish and despair, she betrayed her secret to a friend. This friend at once occupied herself in discovering whether the report of the Marquis' engagement was true, and found that it was a mere rumor. A mystery hangs over her next steps; but it is very certain that Piccolomini no sooner returned to Europe than the Marquis became her accepted lover. The mysterious mediumship of the *confidante* is more than suspected.

In a very brief period after her betrothal, the lovely vocalist laid her laurels at the feet of her lover, and exchanged her profession —its excitement, its inspiration, its glories — for a wife's devotion and a mother's joys.

Few women, famed or unfamed, are so bounteously blessed. She has a charming-home, the most tender and devoted of husbands, three lovely children, admiring friends without number ; sheh as youth, health, wealth, beauty ; but — but — it is useless to deny a fact that is so apparent : though she is happy, though no one can doubt her happiness, there are moments when she pines for her artist life ; a sense of listlessness and of overwhelming *idleness* oppresses her ; her everyday existence does not rouse and stimulate her mind ; does not meet the requirements of her artistic nature. She is often the victim of *ennui ;* often grows dull, as with a surfeit of happiness. When her talents are called into play for charities, she suddenly revives ; a new soul seems breathed into her inanimate frame ; once more she is inspired ; she lives ; she is the Piccolomini of old.

A few seasons ago, her former manager, Mr. Lumley, was in great tribulation, and on the brink of ruin. Piccolomini persuaded her husband to take her to London, and to allow her to play an engagement for the benefit of her old director. There can be no question of the double happiness she experienced —the joy of serving an old and esteemed friend, and the delight of once more revelling in the exercise of her great gifts. Speak of that engagement, and her blue eyes fill with a lustre that rarely illumines them, except when she is singing; her whole face beams, her lips grow tremulous, and her words are broken by suppressed sighs.

The last time she appeared in public in Florence was in November, 1864, at a concert given in aid of the sufferers from the inundation.

She has always been subject to stage fright, and this terrible nightmare is increased by even a brief retirement from the stage. On the occasion of which we speak, when she was summoned to appear, she trembled visibly, from head to foot. She could scarcely breathe, and was seized with a violent palpitation of the heart. When she entered upon the stage her agitation was so overpowering, that she could hardly stand, and she had to grasp a piano, which stood near, for support. She was to sing Donizetti's "*Affandonno*," and to be accompanied on the harp by her master, the distinguished Romanelli, of the Pergola. Almost with the first notes she uttered her terror vanished. The blood rushed back to her pallid cheeks and lips; her eyes flashed and dilated; she stood erect, sublime in her inspired beauty. She sang with vehement passion; she had forgotten herself; she had forgotten all but her divine art; the music in her hand was crumpled, nearly torn, by her nervous fingers; her soul came down into her body, and almost grew visible to mortal eyes.

Her husband sat behind the scenes, not far from our own seat, and where we could watch his face.

It was a picture worth studying. Even so he must have looked in those days in Rome, when his eyes were fastened upon that unknown Piccolomini who was now his wife.

I have already given an account of the frightful inundation, and of the sufferers for whose relief Piccolomini was drawn from her seclusion; and her noble-hearted charity.

THE BEAUTIFUL HORROR.

EVERY one knows that Florence, the gem of Italian cities, is encompassed for miles by grand old villas, dotting lovely valleys and cresting undulating hills. Linked to many of these ancient villas are strange legends — histories of wrong and revenge, of shame and grief, of heroic endurance and cruel martyrdom. One of the most startling of these narratives is associated with the villa *Salviati*, on the road to the picturesque hill of *Fiesole*, a little beyond the villa Careggi, where Lorenzo the Magnificent lived and died.

The superb villa Salviati is now owned by singers of world-wide fame, and as one gazes upon the handsome portraits that adorn its walls, it is from the noble features of the Italian lyric queen that the eye turns to rest upon a face full of bitterness and woe — a face that has the look of one unloved, yet capable of love, and of desperate deeds through that love — the portrait of the Lady Veronica, a daughter of the royal house of Massa, the wife of Jacopo Salviati, Duke of San Guliano, to whom the villa belonged.

Towards the middle of the seventeenth century, there was a grand festival celebrated at this magnificent villa, the last ever given there by a Salviati. The host, then a dashing cavalier in the first flush of reckless manhood, was a few years younger than his wife. She could hardly have been thirty, but the disparity of their ages was rendered striking by the gay *insouciance* of Jacopo Salviati's handsome, furrowless face, and the stern intensity, the wistful eagerness of gaze, that was wearing sharp lines in the countenance of the Lady Veronica.

It was during this feast that one of the spies whom she employed to watch her husband's movements delivered to her a small package. The evening was far advanced. Some of the guests had departed; others lingered upon the threshold, to enjoy the glorious panorama revealed by the rising moon. The Duchess could hardly conceal her impatience to have them gone. She started when the horse of the Duke was brought to the door, and her knitted brow grew visibly darker. Salviati, with smiling suavity, made his apologies to the remaining guests; the

Grand Duke, his master, required his immediate presence.

"The Grand Duke has need of you at *this* hour?" the Duchess whispered, or rather hissed out between her closed teeth.

"Why not?" answered Salviati, aloud. "All my hours are at his command."

He bowed courteously, sprang into the saddle, and waved his hand in graceful adieu as he rode rapidly from the door.

Even while he was speaking, the lady's fingers clutched the little package she had hidden in her pocket, and as she forced her white lips into a sort of smile, and strung unmeaning words together in idle talk, she could not relax her hold.

The last guest turned to depart; then, without a second's pause, the casket tightly grasped in her trembling hands, she flew up the broad stair to her sumptuous chamber. A child, sleeping beneath a canopy of cerulean silk, was wakened by her sudden entrance, and lifted up its little face, flushed with the roses of sleep, and watched her with great, wondering blue eyes, like his father's. She pressed the spring of the morocco case, and shivering, gasping, gazed wildly upon something within. It was a countenance of child-like loveliness, shining out from amid the wealth of loosened tresses, as through a cloud which the sunset had turned to gold. The eyes were blue, and had that pleadingly pathetic expression which told they had early been familiar with sorrow, though they seemed formed only to brighten with joy. And there was the long, slender throat, slender to a fault, which she had so often heard Salviati admire as an especial charm in womanhood. The Duchess raised her eyes; a mirror opposite reflected her own dark, pain-distorted face, her sunken, lustreless eyes, her thick, ungraceful throat. With a look of passionate despair, and a fierce cry, she flung down the miniature and stamped upon it, and tossed her arms above her head, and wheeling round as she staggered towards the bed, suddenly faced the amazed boy.

"Oh, mamma, you frighten me!" he cried; "oh, don't! How ugly you look, mamma!"

The word "ugly" had scarcely passed the child's lips, when she struck him upon the mouth.

"Ugly! Ugly! Do I not know it? Do I not see it? Must even my own child tell me so?"

Then she wept violently, and caught the boy in her arms, and caressed him with a sort of savage remorse until his sobs were hushed.

In the street called *Via dei Pelastri*, near the church *San Ambrosio*, stands the house of Giustino

Canacci, one of the most wealthy, most highly honored, of Florentine merchants.

It is past midnight, but Caterina Canacci sits in the great salon, in the attitude of one listening for distant sounds — sits with an air of expectation. She goes to the window, and looks out, and listens. The moon has disappeared, the heavens have grown dark, threatening one of those sudden storms so common in Italy. She moves to a door at the further end of the apartment, and bends her head to catch the sound from within — the low, regular breathing of one asleep. She softly opens the door, and though the taper burns faintly, it gives light enough to show the benignant features of an old man — the white locks lying upon the pillow, the mild lips parted with a half smile, almost the smile of a sleeping child, it speaks such absence of care, such sweetness of repose.

Caterina closes the door noiselessly, for she has heard a light signal, and flits across the spacious apartment, down the great stair, cautiously lifts the chains of the hall door, and draws back the bolt. A cavalier enters, and is joyfully greeted.

"Jacopo, how bravely you are attired to-night!" she exclaimed with child-like admiration, examining his gala dress. "Come in, step softly; he has only just fallen asleep."

Chains and bolts are replaced, and the lovers pass up the stair, and enter the apartment Caterina has just quitted. They sit side by side, and while the visitor twines his fingers in and out among the loosened tangles of those soft, bright locks, Caterina prattles to him. Some chance word has touched a chord that has opened her heart, and she is telling of grinding poverty, of hard struggles, of the goodness of Giustino Canacci, who came one day to bid her wear his name with a ring, that he might save her and her kindred from further misery. She loved him for his goodness, she said, and then sorrowfully added, Was she not wrong to permit this gay cavalier to visit her so often, and very wrong to have given him her word to hide those visits from her husband? Besides, how little she knew of the cavalier himself. Nothing but that his name was "Jacopo," and that he looked the noblest gentleman she ever saw. And how had he come to notice her, or she him? Only from seeing each other day after day, as she sat at the casement. She had not meant to drop the flower — indeed she had not — which fell from her hands one day, and which he picked up and gained admission to return; though, after all, he did not give it back, as he well knew. How strange that, from that hour to this, he had come so often, and yet she knew nothing about him!

"Except that he loves you!" replied he, fervently.

Caterina put a rosy finger on his lips, and with the other hand pointing to the chamber where the old man slept, answered reproachfully: "I am his, you know; and you promised never to utter words which I could not hear without a blush, or remember without remorse."

The sky had grown darker and darker, and at that moment a sudden peal of thunder shook the old mansion to its base; then came the quick flash and the crashing peal, followed by another and another as violent.

In the silence that ensued, a feeble voice could be heard calling "Caterina! Caterina!" and there was a sound as of one rising from bed, and groping about the chamber with feeble steps.

Caterina started up, trembling helplessly; but the cavalier, with presence of mind, extinguished the lamp.

"Caterina! Caterina!" and the advancing steps were still heard.

A vivid flash, for a second, flooded the whole room as with daylight, and they saw the old man standing, like a spectre, in the doorway, as plainly as he saw Caterina, pale and cowering, and the handsome cavalier bending over her.

"Caterina! Caterina!" almost wailed the old man; "I did not think thou couldst be false to me. Why hast thou done this?"

The tone was one of agony, but not of reproach.

Another flash revealed the three again. The old man staggered forward with one arm outstretched toward the cavalier, as though trying to speak. All was dark again, but they heard a heavy fall, and the next flash showed Giustino Canacci prostrate on the ground.

Caterina darted towards him, and fell on her knees. "Signor! Signor!" she sobbed out, "I have erred, but I have not wronged thee, as thou thinkest. I am not false! Pity me! pity me!"

The Duke had lighted the lamp. He raised the old man in his strong arms and bore him to the bed. Canacci was not insensible; he looked *inquiringly, not angrily*, into the stranger's face, and murmured feebly, "Who art thou?"

Jacopo did not answer.

The dying eyes turned to the weeping Caterina. "Poor lamb! if I took thee to my fold, it was because I knew it would not be for long — it was only to shelter thee."

. "And oh! how ill I have repaid thee; but only in hiding that Jacopo came to see me, and that — that—"

"That he loved thee," replied the old man; and his lips tried impotently to form themselves into a smile. "So be it! I only ask that he will guard thee tenderly. I shall not make him wait."

He laid the soft little hand which was clasping his in that of the cavalier, who took it in silence. A sharp pang choked his utterance, but if he could have spoken, was it possible to tell the old man that he could not wear this jewel upon his breast? Was it possible to slay Caterina with that knowledge in such an hour? Some good angel prompted him to do so, even then, and save her and himself; but the opportunity was soon lost. Caterina was bending over a corpse, wildly lamenting, and accusing herself of having caused the death of her benefactor.

––––

The events just narrated took place early in November. Upon New Year's Eve, a heavy fall of snow, very rare in Florence, kept almost all Italians within doors, for they ever shrink from cold. The snow rendered noiseless the steps of those who ventured forth, and deadened even the sound of carriage wheels.

Two men, shrouded in long cloaks, were hiding, in the *Via dei Pelastri*, near the house where Giustino Canacci had dwelt. Once or twice they stole from their place of concealment, as though to reconnoitre, and looked down the street. If a stray foot passenger chanced to get a glimpse of them, he quickened his pace with a shudder. The trade of the assassin was well known in Florence, but no one dared to meddle with another seeking for vengeance.

A carriage approached noiselessly. The man who was playing the part of coachman was evidenly unused to such an office; he drew up awkwardly a few paces beyond Canacci's former residence. A lady, wearing a black mask, looked out for a moment, when the carriage stopped, then spoke in a whisper to one within. There was no answer, but a man put forth his hand, opened the door, leapt out, and walked boldly up to the dark angle where the two bravoes were hiding. This man was in no way disguised, except by the fumes of liquor, which usually enveloped him, and brought to the surface the most brutish part of his nature. Almost any passer by would have recognized him as Masso, a low, lawless fellow, the only son of Giustino Canacci by a first marriage.

He had never looked with favorable eyes upon the pretty Caterina, but when he learned that the bulk of his father's large fortune was left to her, only an Italian can conceive how he hated her, and how open he was to overtures from those who shared that hatred.

Masso exchanged a few words with the men and then returned to the carriage.

"Signora, he has not gone yet."

The lady did not reply, but signalled to him to resume his seat in the coach.

They had not waited long when the door of Giustino Canacci's house opened, and the lamp, carried by a beautiful girl attired in mourning, fell upon the radiant face of a cavalier who was carefully enveloping himself in his cloak. As he passed the threshold he turned and tenderly kissed her forehead.

The lady, who was leaning far out of the carriage, drew back and clinched her hands until the nails pierced the flesh and blood marked the pressure of every finger.

The cavalier went rapidly on his way. As soon as he was out of sight, Masso again descended from the carriage, and knocked at the door. Caterina had not had time to return to her apartment, for it was her voice that answered, without opening, "Who is there?"

"It is I — Masso; open the door."

The order was at once obeyed.

"Come to the salon: I have something to say to you," said Masso.

Caterina, bearing the light, led the way to the salon, having first carefully closed the door.

When they entered the room, Masso said:

"Wait for me here a moment — I have forgotten something."

Caterina nodded a smiling assent, and seated herself. Masso returned to the street, handed the lady from the carriage, and signalled the two bravoes. All four entered the house, and the door was closed and barred. Masso led the way to the apartment where Caterina sat. The masked lady entered first; the three men grouped themselves near the entrance, but she strode up to Caterina.

"What is this? Who are you, madam?" inquired Caterina, somewhat startled, though not evincing any great alarm.

The lady removed her mask.

"Do you not know me?"

"No, truly, Signora," answered Caterina; but her voice trembled, for the satanic expression of the woman who stood before her might well have terrified a braver heart.

"I am the wife of the Duke San Giuliano."

Caterina did not change color; she simply bowed,

and her blue eyes looked the inquiry she was too courteous to speak.

"Who left this house a few moments ago?" asked the Duchess.

Caterina did not answer.

"It was *your lover!*" shrieked the Duchess.

Caterina dropped her eyelids silently, but without shame; she had no thought of denying the fact.

"The Duke. San Giuliano?" added the Duchess, fiercely.

Then Caterina gave a violent start, and her face blanched·with terror, as she exclaimed, —

"No! no! Oh, no!"

"I tell you *yes* — I saw him? My eyes are not false as *he is*, and as *you are!*"

Caterina's limbs refused to support her, and she dropped, half kneeling, half crouching, before the Duchess.

"You mistook — you mistook! Jacopo, who left me but now, has no wife. When I put off these weeds he will have one. He has told me a hundred times that he never loved any woman save me. It was the *truth*, I knew. You have mistaken him for some one else."

Then the lady's fury burst all bounds. She sprang toward the girl, and seizing her by the throat — that beautiful throat, which her husband must have thought of when he so landed slender throats — plunged her dagger in Caterina's breast, exclaiming, —

"*Two* wives he cannot have! *Thus* I rid him of the one whom he dared to say he loved! He has only one left to love."

The wound was not mortal, and Caterina, with the strength of fear, struggled to her feet, and freed herself from the grasp of the frantic woman — but she encountered the bravoes!

. . . .

Masso went forth to see that her cries had not been heard. The men soon followed him.

After a long interval the door opened again, and the lady appeared. She carried in her hand a small black bag, entered the carriage, laid the bag on her knees, and held it there as she was driven back to the Villa Salviati.

———

The Duke woke early the next morning, and summoned his valets. It was New Year's Day, and all the world would throng the court to pay homage to the sovereign. Salviati bade his valets bring forth his most costly attire. He was merry that morning, and liberal because he was merry; he flung to each a large piece of gold to celebrate the

"*Capo 'd Anno*" (New Year), for it was a year which promised *much happiness*, he said. He was humming a popular love song, when some one tapped lightly on the door.

"Come in!"

A servant entered, bearing a blue velvet basket, embroidered with seed pearls, and apparently well filled with fine cambric. The cavaliers of those days delighted in fine linen and rich laces.

"My lady sends to my lord Duke this New Year's gift."

"Thank your lady, and say I wish her a happy New Year. This is for thee." He tossed the attendant a piece of gold.

The laces were very costly. Upon the top lay a superb handkerchief; then came a rich collar and cuffs; he was trying to lift out the next article, but the lace must have caught — it appeared to be fastened. He plunged his hand in the basket to loosen it. His fingers came in contact with something very soft and silky; the touch, *though familiar*, thrilled him like an electric shock. He drew out his hand, but, tangled about the fingers, was a long, long tress of burnished gold. Terror stricken, he tore away the cambric which covered something in the bottom of the basket. *Oh, beautiful horror!* that face — the delicate features white as wax,

10*

the sightless, glassy, blue eyes, opened wide — the head of his beautiful Caterina lay before him!

With the savage roar of a wild beast, Salviati rushed from the apartment to that of his wife.

The Duchess was gone. She had only returned home the night previous, prepared that basket, left it in charge of a servant, and fled.

The false husband and revengeful wife never met again. Salviati, after wandering about the world, resting nowhere, and finding no peace, haunted by that beautiful horror, died in his prime.

Veronica took up her residence at her father's court. Often and often she prayed for pardon; but Salviati was deaf to her supplications. Her life dragged on to extreme old age. She passed her days in acts of charity, which brought comfort to other hearts, but hers was evermore comfortless.

GINEVRA.

THERE is an antique street in Florence, running from the *Piazza del Duomo* to the *Via del Oche*, which bears the startling title of *Via della Morta* — Street of the Dead. The original name of *Via del Campanile* was changed to *Via della Morta* to commemorate the resuscitation of the beautiful Ginevra, who, having escaped from the tomb, wandered through the streets by night, seeking that shelter which the terrors of superstition denied her.

The story of Ginevra, even more thrilling and singularly romantic than that of Romeo and Juliet, or *Ippolito Buondelmonte* and *Dianora dei Bardi* (whom T. Adolphus Trollope styles the " *Tuscan* Romeo and Juliet"), can hardly be called a tradition or legend. It is, beyond question, a true history, and has been chronicled by various reliable Italian historians — *Lastri, Rondinelli, del Migliori;* but the most minute account is that given by Manni in his " *Veglie Piacevole.*"

Leigh Hunt has incorporated some of the chief incidents of the life of Ginevra in his drama entitled " A Legend of Florence;" a play which was enacted at the Theatre Royal, Covent Garden, 1840, when the *rôle* of Ginevra was exquisitely personated by Miss Ellen Tree.

The distinguished author has, however, made a most unaccountable error in regard to the period in which Ginevra lived. According to the above-mentioned historians, the most remarkable event of her life occurred in 1396, but Leigh Hunt states the time of his play to be " during the Pontificate of Leo X." Pope Leo X. was not born until 1475, and he did not become Pope until more than a century after the death of Ginevra. Strange to say, Leigh Hunt does not seem to have been acquainted with some of the most striking features of her history. If he had been, he could hardly have omitted in his play an element so highly dramatic as the citing of Ginevra and her early lover, *Antonio Rondinelli*, before the tribunal of her enraged husband, *Francesco degli Agolanti;* Ginevra's eloquent recital of her wrongs; the wonder and sympathy of the Florentine public, and the extraordinary decision of the judges.

The Rondinelli were a very ancient and much-esteemed Florentine family. They gave to the Republic thirty-six *Priori*, twelve *Gonfalonieri* (mayors), and one Senator, or *Commendatore*. The name *Rondinelli* signifies *swallow*, and the *Rondinelli* coat-of-arms was a swallow upon a field of gold.

Towards the close of the fourteenth century, the young *Antonio Rondinelli* became enamored of *Ginevra degli Almieri*, a lady of high lineage. Bernardo, the father of Ginevra, a stern, hard, grasping man, was at variance with the Rondinelli family (an occurrence almost too common between noble Florentine families, in those days, to be worthy of mention). The youthful Ginevra warmly responded to the passion her lovely person and lovelier character had kindled; and notwithstanding the division between their families, the trusting lovers basked in the delicious hope that they would one day be united.

Antonio sought Bernardo degli Almieri, and in spite of a frigid and frowning reception, boldly avowed his affection for Ginevra, and prayed that the discord between their houses might be melted into harmony by her fair hand, clasped, before the altar, in his. The father repulsed him rudely, and forbade all intercourse between the lovers. Then Ginevra, gaining courage through her dismay, went to her father and implored him to hear her — told

him of her love for Antonio, and besought him not
to separate them. Her father turned an obdurate
ear to her pleadings, and drove her from his presence. Ginevra mourned and pined for her banished lover without disguising her sorrow. Bernardo augured from this open grief that she cherished a hope that he would be moved to revoke the
sentence of separation. To dispel any such base-
less delusion, he determined to give her in marriage
without delay.

Francesco degli Agolanti was one of the most
opulent men in Florence. From certain facts, however, related by historians, it may be inferred that
he was as miserly as he was wealthy. Ginevra, far
from listening to his wooing, turned from him with
unconcealed aversion; but this did not prevent
Agolanti's demanding her hand of her father, who
promised it willingly. When her approaching
betrothal was announced to Ginevra, she made resolute resistance, and conjured her imperious father
not to add this new affliction to the one which had
already bereft her of her happiness. His reply was
to hasten the preparations for her nuptials. When
Ginevra found her struggles fruitless, she fell into
a state of deep dejection and listless apathy. She
no longer seemed to notice what passed around her,
and was led to the altar unresistingly, as though her

faculties had become torpid — as if she was no longer capable even of the sensation of pain.

After her marriage, this inert and passive condition became confirmed. She moved about like a being whose soul was absent, and went through the ordinary routine of life mechanically, almost unconsciously. She seldom spoke, or smiled, or even lamented her fate aloud. Very soon she was attacked by an hysterical affection which induced long swoons of frequent occurrence. The physicians who attended her pronounced her disease consumption. At the end of four years, she one day fell into a swoon, from which all efforts to revive her proved ineffectual. The medical men, after having exhausted their skill without result, informed her husband that she had expired.

At sunset on the evening of the same day, she was carried, with great pomp, upon an open funeral car, to the family vault of the Agolanti in the cemetery of the *Duomo.* Here, according to custom, her fair body was laid upon a shelf, 'among the mouldering skeletons of her husband's ancestors. The month was October. The moon shone brightly that night. The stone placed at the mouth of the tomb had not been re-cemented. The masons were to perform the work on the morrow. Through the aperture left by the loosened and ill-fitting stone, the moonlight streamed, and lighted up the dismal vault.

Ginevra from her long swoon had sunk into a deep trance, but life was not extinct. In the middle of the night she feebly stirred, and slowly recovered her consciousness. At first, in her half-wakened and tremulously weak state, she thought herself oppressed by a frightful dream. But as her senses fully returned, she saw the skeleton forms with which she was holding companionship, and attempted to start up, but fell back powerless and in great affright; for she now discovered that her hands and feet were bound. Then, for the first time, she beheld the grave-clothes in which she was attired, and knew by them, and her bandaged feet and hands, that she must have been supposed to be dead, and had been buried. Fear lent her new strength, and after many despairing efforts she succeeded in loosening the bandages, and disentangling herself from the swathing folds of her long shroud. She stood up, trembling and appalled, but, guided by the moonlight, staggered to the five steps before the entrance, and crept up to the stone which barred her exit. To remove it with those delicate and feeble hands seemed impossible; but at such moments the frailest natures are endowed with superhuman strength. After several futile attempts, which with every failure increased her horror, the stone was rolled over, and she stood in the moonlight, in the open cemetery, freed — saved from a living tomb, probably from a death of maddening terror.

With feeble steps she hurried through the streets, her long shroud trailing on the ground, her white drapery floating around her, and her ghastly face looking unearthly in the moonlight. She was seeking her home — the home from which she had that morning been borne as a corpse. What wonder that the midnight stragglers who met her thought that they saw an apparition, and fled affrighted?

At last she reached Francesco Agolanti's house, in the street called by the name of his family, and, knocking, sank upon the threshold, crying out to her husband to admit her quickly. The window of Agolanti's chamber opened upon a balcony which commanded the front entrance. He heard the knock and the pleading cry, and hastened to the balcony. Ginevra looked up, and called to him with a feeble, imploring voice. He recognized the grave-shrouded form, the white face, and the plaintive tones, and was seized with frantic alarm, for he believed himself visited by the ghost of his buried wife. Making the sign of the cross repeatedly, and with great rapidity and vehemence, he bade her depart and

leave him in peace, promising that abundant masses
should be said for the rest of her soul. Ginevra, in
an agonized voice, replied that she lived, and entreated to be admitted. Her husband, more terrified
than ever, rushed into his chamber, closed the
window, sprang into bed, and covering his head
with the clothes, to shut out the terrible sound of
that low, piteous plaint, recited the *De Profundis*
until all was silent again.

The hapless Ginevra rose from the ground with
difficulty, and with tottering feet dragged herself
to the door of her father's house in the *Mercato
Vecchio*, behind *S. Andrea*. Again she knocked,
and prayed to be allowed to come in ; but when
her summons roused the domestics, and her father
himself, she was again mistaken for an apparition ;
the door was closed upon her, and her father and
his servants retreated in alarm. Ginevra lay upon
the cold steps, almost insensible, and in despair. All
who saw her fled, terror-stricken, from her presence.
She had returned from the grave, and no one would
grant her earthly shelter.

No one? Was there not *one* who would never
bid her depart, even should he imagine that she had
come to him as a spirit ? With that thought she
once more struggled to her feet, and made her toil-

some way through the deserted streets to the *Piazza San Lorenzo*, where dwelt Antonio Rondinelli.

Antonio still loved her with unabated ardor, and had taken a vow to be constant to her memory, and never to marry. The tidings of her death had reached him, and he had not sought his couch that night. He was sitting weeping, and thinking of his doubly lost Ginevra.

Her strength was now so far exhausted, that she could only knock very feebly; but Antonio heard the sound, and passing out into his balcony, saw the grave-clad figure, and the upturned, colorless face of Ginevra. She faintly murmured his name. He, too, believed that it was a spirit — but it was the spirit of his beloved, and the sight and sound filled him with transport. Rapidly and joyfully he descended, and threw open the entrance door, and stooped to raise the cold, shrouded form that lay prostrate at his feet. What painter, what poet could picture his amazement and his ecstasy? Ginevra lived, and was restored to him !

He summoned his mother, with whom he resided, and assembled his family to rejoice with him, and to listen to Ginevra's tale. Then Antonio bound them all by an oath to silence, and sent a faithful servant to replace the stone upon the opening of the vault, and to remove every trace of the fugitive's footsteps. Meantime the exhausted Ginevra, now indeed almost dying from the neglect and hardships she had endured, was laid in a warm bed, and tenderly ministered to by the mother of Antonio. For four days Ginevra's life seemed like a flickering candle, which a single breath might extinguish. On the fifth day she gradually revived, and before long was able to rise and converse.

She then pondered deeply and sadly upon the only honorable course that was left to her, and with gentle firmness announced to Antonio, that, as she could never return to her brutal husband's protection, she felt herself compelled to enter a convent. Antonio, hurled from his sudden happiness into an abyss of despair, implored her to revoke this cruel decision — cruel not to him only, but to herself. He brought forward manifold arguments to convince her that the tie which bound her to Agolanti was dissolved by a death and burial which all the world believed to be real, and entreated her to become the wife of one who had never loved but her, and had claimed her for his own before she was sold to Agolanti. His mother and family joined their prayers to his, and Ginevra listening to them, and to the pleadings of her own heart, slowly consented.

It is recorded that Antonio and Ginevra were

privately united by the public notary, who was bound to secrecy.

Meantime all Florence was listening to descriptions of the ghost of Ginevra, which so many persons had beheld passing through the streets, and which her husband testified had appeared to him, and her father made known had also visited his door. The two families ordered a bountiful number of masses to be said for the repose of the unquiet spirit.

Agolanti now offered the jewels and wardrobe of Ginevra for sale. His great wealth did not prevent his evincing this lack of reverence for her memory, impelled by a sordid love of gain. Rondinelli, as soon as he heard of the proposed barter, hastened to the residence of Agolanti, and purchased every article his newly-made wife had possessed, paying the most extravagant prices to prevent the smallest object which had been consecrated by her use from passing into the hands of strangers.

For some months Ginevra lived in entire seclusion, her existence unknown to any but her husband's family and a few trustworthy domestics. But neither she nor her husband were satisfied with this mode of life. Rondinelli saw no reason why he should not appear before the world as the proud husband of so fair and beloved a wife. Ginevra, too, detested the constant stratagems to which they were obliged to resort, and resolved to go forth boldly. In the revivifying atmosphere of calm happiness and satisfied love, she had risen out of the passive inertness which had paralyzed her faculties during the four miserable years which she had passed under the roof of Agolanti, and her character reassumed its genuine traits. Frank, ardent, and confident, hating dissimulation, and having firm faith that the step she had taken was fully justified, she exhibited neither fear nor hesitation, and was ready to brave the ordeal of public opinion.

Accordingly, one morning, Antonio and Ginevra were seen in the Boboli Gardens. Ginevra was leaning on her husband's arm, his sister accompanied them, and a servant followed. They encountered friends, whose amazement rendered them almost speechless. But Ginevra, whenever she saw she was recognized, paused, and courteously addressed her former acquaintances. She told them that her husband had not only hastily buried her alive, without the proper investigation which might have proved that she was not dead, but that when she sought his door, and that of her father, she had been rejected by both; and that it was not the fault of husband, father, priests, or physicians that she was not in reality dead; for dead she must

The Boboli Gardens and rear view of Palazzo Pitti; Florence.—*Page* 238.

shortly have been but for him who alone had truly loved her, and opened his door and his arms to receive her, whether she came in the flesh or the spirit; and therefore it was to him that her life belonged, and to him it had been consecrated.

Francesco degli Agolanti soon heard of his wife's re-appearance, of her defiant words and her new marriage. Finding that the tale was true, he made an appeal (with *great clamor*, as the Italian historians say) to the courts of justice, to induce them to restore Ginevra to him, her rightful husband.

Ginevra and Antonio were summoned to appear before the ecclesiastical court, over which the archbishop presided. The excitement ran high throughout Florence, and the court was surrounded by an indignant and enthusiastic populace, who denounced Agolanti and Bernardo, and openly declared their sympathy for Antonio and Ginevra. Before the tribunal Ginevra told her tale bravely and with great feeling, and made known her determination to resist her former husband's effort to reclaim her, after he had twice placed her life in peril, had shut her up in the grave, and had closed his doors upon her; adding, that if she should be separated from Antonio, she would take refuge from Agolanti in a convent.

The cause was ably argued on both sides. But

the judges, in those times, hardly dared to gainsay the outspoken verdict of the many-mouthed public, which was apt to decide for them what was justice, and to enforce that justice, when not summarily dealt out, by riot and bloodshed.

The decision given will seem almost incredible in our days. The marriage between Agolanti and Ginevra was declared void and null, through her supposed death and actual burial; and the court decided that she was free to form other ties, according to her good pleasure; that the ties she had contracted were legal; and that she was now the lawful wife of Antonio Rondinelli!

LA BELLE CLEMENTINE.

PART I.

" *La Belle Clementine !* "   That was the only name by which she was known when she stood before the French tribunal — the only name by which she is designated on the records of the criminal court of Paris.   The French law makes a lenient provision by which a culprit's family is spared undeserved shame, and thus the real name of " *La Belle Clementine,*" throughout her trial, was kept a profound secret.

Clementine belonged to one of those noble, but decayed, families, whose exclusiveness had not survived its wealth.   It was not difficult to obtain admission into the *salons* which the degenerate nobility frequented.   The handsome, daring, dashing *Chevalier de la Rocheforte* found an easy *entrée,* and nobody troubled himself about the *Chevalier's* antecedents.

" *La Belle Clementine* " had hardly completed

her seventeenth year when they met. De la Rocheforte was quickly and genuinely enamored of the
peerless beauty, and Clementine was too impassion-
ate, imaginative, ardent, not to be captivated in
turn.

Her beauty was all the more striking, because
wholly unlike the French type. Those changeful
eyes, the positive color of which might have been
gray, but appears now blue, now violet, now hazel, and
now black; that luxuriant hair, revealing a variety
of tints — bright chestnut near the roots, and the
hue of satiny straw towards the ends; the finely
shaped nostrils, that expand when the eye dilates;
the transparent skin, that shows the delicate veins
beneath, betrays the faintest blush of emotion, and
renders pallor more marble-like when the blood re-
treats — these were eloquent signs of the temperament most dangerous to womanhood before its ears
are opened to the heaven-commissioned monitor
within.

For the Chevalier de la Rocheforte to have offered
himself openly as a suitor to Clementine, would
have entailed the necessity of making known his
birth, his means of livelihood, his actual position;
and there were very good reasons why these should
remain enveloped in mystery. Singular as it may
seem, vanity, and perhaps a touch of latent honesty,

prompted him to test the depth of Clementine's infatuation, and the struggle of his own power, by thrilling her ears with the romantic narrative of his lawless youth, and the history of daring exploits, to which the administrators of justice would have given a somewhat sterner name.

Did Clementine shrink from the man who stood before her an avowed criminal? Alas! it is as sad as true, that a large class of women are subject to a sort of demoniacal possession which takes the form of frantic admiration for a villain-hero. The awe, dread, and wonder, and with which they regard these fascinating demi-devils, only strengthen the unreasoning passion. Clementine, when she heard from her lover's own lips the story of his unworthiness, was more madly in love with him than before. She was ready to fly with him, to cling to him, to share his dangers and be covered with his shame, to risk life itself by his side.

A secret union in France was out of the question for one who had not reached her majority. They fled to England, where the marriage was duly solemnized, returned to Paris, and lived in seclusion, undiscovered by her relatives.

Three years after "*La Belle Clementine*" became the wife of "*Victorien le Victorieux*," as he was styled by the band of ruffians whom he ruled with a rod of iron, and who idolized him for his bravery, a robbery was committed on the premises of a wealthy miser, followed by murder — a murder which was supposed to have been unintentional, and perpetrated in self-defence. The offenders were traced to the abode of their chief; Victorien and his band were arrested, and with them "*La Belle Clementine.*"

The trial lasted many days, and though it took place with "closed doors," very little influence was needed to obtain admission, and the court was thronged.

Clementine's remarkable beauty, her youth, her apparent unsophistication, and her passionate attempts to shield her husband, moved even her judges to compassion. Victorien and several of his comrades were found guilty of murder, and sentenced to the guillotine; "*La Belle Clementine*" and the others were condemned to imprisonment for life.

Clementine was thrown into a state of frenzy by the sentence passed upon her husband, and piteously implored to be allowed to share his fate; since the judges thought her guilty, let the guillotine be her doom also; the sentence they had passed on her was no punishment — for if Victorien died, the whole world would be but one vast, solitary prison-house, which their sentence could not render more desolate.

Her pathetic appeal was not one to be granted, but it heightened the agitation visible throughout the court. That emotion had in one instance been so violent, that when the jury pronounced the verdict of "guilty," a young man fell to the ground, and was borne forth insensible.

That night De la Rocheforte swallowed an acid, which he had himself prepared by steeping a sou in vinegar, and was found dead in his cell.

When the tidings were communicated to Clementine, they seemed to benumb her intellect; she sank into a state of physical and mental prostration, and was hardly conscious of her removal to the *Maison Centrale* at *Fontevrault*. An attack of brain fever ensued, and when she rallied, her body alone appeared to have returned to life — her soul remained afar off.

Happily she found a pitying friend in the kindly physician of the prison. He advised her to petition to be sent to Cayenne, where she would at least have more freedom, be allowed to breathe the fresh air, and have duties assigned her which would help to divert her thoughts from brooding over the miserable past and dreary future. Clementine, grateful for any change, and believing that none could be for the worse, made the application. The request was granted without difficulty, and the stricken, doomed, desolate girl made a tedious voyage to the French penal settlement in South America, which is a less intolerable home to the convict than the prisons of France. On the small, arid, sun-scorched island of Cayenne, Clementine thought to pass the remainder of her days.

PART II.

WE have already mentioned that when "*La Belle Clementine*" was pronounced guilty, there was one person among the sympathizing crowd so strongly moved that he fell prostrate and unconscious. It was the Viscount Eugéne de Rosier, a youth of eighteen. Every day, while the trial lasted, he had presented himself at the doors long before they were opened, and, being the first to enter, he always made his way to the same seat — one where he could face the prisoners at the bar. His agitation when *La Belle Clementine* appeared in the dock was often so uncontrollable, that it drew the eyes of the court upon him. When appearances seemed to criminate her, he clenched his hands, gasped for breath, and sometimes tore open his vest as if he were stifling. His eager eyes never turned from her face, and now and then it seemed as though magnetically they drew her eyes to look his way. In leaving the court he was often heard asserting his firm belief in her innocence, quoting circumstances which proved that she could not be guilty, and vehemently protesting that her only crime consisted in loving too faithfully and too blindly a villain.

Friends inquired if the young Viscount knew "*La Belle Clementine*" personally. "Know her? Yes, — No," he answered, incoherently. That is, he knew her; for who could listen to all those minute details of her life, and feel that he did not know her? Who could look upon her wondrously beautiful countenance until it became so familiar that it filled his mental vision night and day, and say that he did not know her? But, except before that dreadful tribunal, they had never met; he had never addressed one word to her; and yet he was sure she knew of his sympathy, his devotion, his prayers that she might be proved innocent. Their eyes had met'— she had thanked him by a grateful look — had told him of her innocence by the indignant flush that mantled her cheek when she was accused. No jury would dare to commit such a wrong as to find a verdict of "guilty" against her.

When the last day of the trial came—when he discovered his error, and heard that appalling word pronounced, the young Viscount started from his seat, trembling, and deadly pale. He strove to speak, but the words turned into a hoarse cry, which broke the solemn stillness that followed the verdict. Then came the sound of a fall, and all eyes, even those of Clementine, the convicted, were turned upon the youth, whom the *gens d'armes* carried insensible from the court.

When he recovered from his swoon, the young Viscount raved wildly against the injustice of the law, declared that he would see Clementine again, would give her the assurance that there was one who would move heaven and earth to get her sentence revoked, or enable her to escape. His friends only laughed at his vague threats, and his parents secretly remarked how well enthusiasm became him —how his eyes glittered with an unwonted light, what a torrent of eloquence burst from his lips. But suddenly Eugéne disappeared. He made no preparations, left no letter, had not supplied himself with money, and his purse was usually empty.

Agonized by terrible fears, his father offered a large reward for his discovery, and he was soon traced by the police. On the road to Fontainebleau they found an exhausted, half-starved youth, whose college dress betrayed him. He had wandered three or four days and nights without food or shelter, determined to reach the *Maison Centrale*, and to see Clementine. He had planned various extravagant modes of obtaining an interview, and he was within sight of the walls of the city, when is over-taxed strength abandoned him, and he sank by the wayside, unable to drag himself a step farther. In spite of his pathetic entreaties to be allowed to complete his journey, he was re-conducted to his home.

It was only too evident that his mind had become seriously unsettled by what French physicians call the *idée fixe*. For years he was kept under the surveillance, first of a tutor, then of a constant companion. Notwithstanding his mental infirmity, he distinguished himself at college. He also excelled in fencing, boxing, running, leaping; he was a daring equestrian, and one of the most skilful swordsmen in Paris; he cultivated all gymnastic exercises with singular perseverance, as though he had some hidden object in view, and expected an hour would come when he would fight against fearful odds, overleap the most most formidable barriers, make his escape, and fly unimpeded by heavy burdens.

His father died, leaving the son but a small patrimony with his title. At last the irritating watchfulness which had thrown a restraint over Eugéne's actions was relaxed. He had always delighted to exhibit his strength of muscle. He suddenly invented a new mode for its display at the Jockey Club, of which he was a member, by bending a Napoleon between his finger and thumb — gold became wax in his iron grip. This feat he performed many times, and after bending the coin, always presented it to one of the wondering lookers-on, and received another Napoleon in exchange.

A young man from Bordeaux, who was making his first visit to Paris, was so much struck by the ease with which Count de Rosier folded up these coins, that he frequently desired him to repeat the experiment, always securing the bent coins as trophies, and giving others in exchange. It chanced, after a time, that the young Bordeaulaise fell short of money, and took the little stock of bent Napoleons which he had kept as curiosities to the money-changers. The information which he received on presenting them caused him to rush to the club in a state of fury. There he found the Count sitting in his usual seat, and in an attitude which had lately become habitual to him — that of a man who

was *waiting*, waiting for some one or something —
always *waiting!*

His face brightened strangely as he saw the
flushed and enraged countenance of the Bordeaulaise, and grew brighter still, when the young man
planted himself in front of the Count, and requested
the gentlemen present to bear witness that every
Napoleon which Count de Rosier had bent with
such marvellous facility, and in exchange for which
he had received good money, was *counterfeit!*

The Count rose, bowed courteously, and replied,
with an air of self-congratulation, " You are right,
sir; they are counterfeit coins, every one of them!
I freely admit the fact."

He spoke in a tone of triumph.

" Sir," exclaimed his exasperated accuser, " do
you know that this is a crime for which I shall bring
you to justice ? "

" You are bound to do so, sir," replied the Count,
complacently.

" Do you suppose that I am jesting, that you take
it so coolly ? " returned the Bordeaulaise. " Are
you aware that you will probably be transported ? "

" Yes — to Cayenne! that is all I ask. Heaven
knows I have done enough to be sent there! But
I have been so unfortunate, nobody would ever find
me out ! "

The gentlemen who had formed a circle around De Rosier looked at each other aghast.

Seeing that no one moved, he asked indignantly:

"Why am I not arrested? Have I not admitted that the coins were false?"

At this crisis an elderly gentleman suggested that the Count should be locked in the room where he then was, and begged the other members of the club to withdraw to an adjoining apartment. When they were assembled there he strenuously advised, that, before sending for the officers of justice, Dr. Blanche, the celebrated physician for the insane, should be summoned.

The Count sat waiting, with that air of eager expectation which had grown so familiar to his features. But when the door opened, and he turned to welcome an officer, he encountered a physician.

After a brief interview, Dr. Blanche informed the members of the club that the unfortunate Count was undoubtedly laboring under monomania, and that his fixed determination to behold and succor a being who had made an indelible impression on his youthful imagination would cause him to commit any act of madness. He added that there was but one chance of cure — a faint one, perhaps, but still chance — and that lay in the gratification of the ardent desire which he had cherished for full twenty years. The Count fancied that in beholding *"La Belle Clementine"* he would see the young and beautiful woman whose image was ever present to his eyes. But twenty years had elapsed. Clementine must now be forty — time, toil, exposure to a tropical sun, and the wretched existence she must have led, had doubtless destroyed her personal charms. The presence of the real being would dethrone the ideal, and dissipate the Count's infatuation. The benevolent doctor concluded by saying that if the members of the club would lend him their aid in taking steps to render this voyage to Cayenne feasible, it might be the means of restoring to reason an unfortunate gentleman whom they had all hitherto esteemed.

Not a man present withheld his consent, and the generous young Bordeaulaise was one of the most zealous in discussing the best method to be adopted, and afterwards in carrying into execution the plans agreed upon.

PART III.

Clementine, by the time she reached Cayenne, was comparatively restored to physical health. She seldom spoke, and never murmured. In a state of stolid abstraction she went mechanically through the labors assigned her — labors for which those small, delicately-moulded hands, that bore witness to her gentle blood, were how unfitted! She was never roused from her apathy, save by the voice of the priest whose duty it was to visit the convicts. She never seemed to experience the faintest emotion, either of pain or pleasure, except when she was assembled with her unfortunate companions to listen to his exhortations; and then it was only the expression of unutterable anguish upon her pallid countenance that betrayed her mental agony.

As years passed on, little by little, a holy calm, full of earnest endeavor, took the place of her apathetic tranquillity; no stranger who looked into those serenely thoughtful eyes could have believed that hers was an existence without earthly hope; that she was a convict for life!

Gradually more liberty was accorded her; she was permitted to nurse the sick, and it was soon found that she ministered to them with singular skill and tenderness. She also evinced a marvellous power to comfort those whom a sentence as severe as her own had driven to reckless despair. She induced them to accept the fate which was inevitable, and to turn their thoughts to that life which was full of hope, even to such as they. Often the most degraded and ungovernable listened to her pleading voice, and their blasphemies and lamentations melted into prayers. She always spoke of herself as of one as guilty as they; and this self-accusation seemed all the stronger from the fact, that the most criminal of her companions were ever striving to prove their innocence and the injustice of their sentence.

From time to time, reports sent from the penal colony to the French Government set forth the piety, and virtue, and untiring zeal of "Clementine." But her sad story had almost passed out of the minds of those who now heard these accounts.

It would be tedious to enter into the full particulars of the movement which resulted in the embarkation of Count Eugéne de Rosier and a young physician, selected by Dr. Blanche, for Cayenne.

Eugéne betrayed no symptoms of derangement during the passage, except, indeed in the enthusiasm with which he over and over again described to his companion the eloquent face, the rapid transitions of expression, the great eyes of changing hue; the hair of mingled tints, so luxuriant in its thick waves and rich curls; the fragile, graceful form, the lofty bearing, the picturesque attire, of "*La Belle Clementine.*" He would know her anywhere, he affirmed;

in any garb; and a voice within told him that she, too, would instantly recognize him.

As they neared the port, he gave way to a wild burst of joy, and his impatience became so great, that Dr. Jouvet placed his arm in that of his patient, and grasped him firmly, fearing that he might plunge into the waves, and endeavor to swim to the shore, for he was a bold and experienced swimmer. They were safely landed at last, and without delay sought the residence of the Governor; were courteously received by him; presented the letter of which Dr. Jouvet was the bearer, and obtained an order for the Count to visit Clementine.

On their way to the prison, Eugéne was filled with dismay at the dreary appearance of the island; at the sight of the wretched, wasted, diseased convicts whom he encountered. Through what horrors "*La Belle Clementine,*" so young, so beautiful, must have passed during her twenty years of captivity! Twenty years! Could it be twenty years since he beheld her last? And he could see her face as vividly, could remember the sound of her voice and the most trivial incidents of that fearful trial as perfectly, as though twenty hours instead of twenty years had elapsed.

Dr. Jouvet delivered the Governor's order to the head matron, and when she retired to summon

Clementine, he also withdrew. Eugéne was left in the rude, bare apartment appropriated to the matron's use, waiting with beating heart and breath almost suspended.

In a few moments the door opened, and he bounded forward impetuously, but stopped; for there stood before him an elderly woman, attired in the uncouth prison dress; her hair smoothed away from her brow and almost entirely concealed beneath an ill-shaped cap; her form very far from fragile; her face round, and somewhat ruddy, though lightly furrowed; and her whole aspect that of an unpretending, self-possessed matron.

The Count paused abruptly, and then said, with an apologetic air:

"I desired to see Clementine — *La Belle* Clementine!" he added, fervently.

The matron's lips did not part even with the faintest *soupçon* of a smile at this familiar appellation. She merely raised her eyes to his face with a look of inquiry; the hue of those steady eyes was not dubious: it was clearly and softly gray. Then, bowing calmly, and without a shadow of emotion, she replied:

"I am Clementine, *Monsieur.*"

"*You!*"

The Count was struck speechless. He gazed at

her in agonized bewilderment; tried to recognize her features, her form, her expression, her voice even — in vain! in vain! He had never seen, never heard, this cold, calm, self-contained matron before.

At last he gasped out:

" And you — *you* remember *me ?* "

" No, Monsieur," was the laconic answer.

" No! and I was there through it all; I watched you every day; I knew you were innocent — innocent of everything, but loving too well."

Clementine started, and flushed crimson; the gray eyes had grown very dark as they were raised heavenward for an instant, and then dropped their lids.

" Through all these years your face has ever been before my eyes," resumed the Count.

Clementine's gaze was bent upon the ground, and, though her lips quivered, she made no answer.

" Say, at least, that you remember the youth who swooned when you were pronounced guilty ? "

She shuddered visibly, and, in a half-whisper, answered :

" Yes, I remember."

" He has dreamed of you night and day ; has followed you here, after all these years, to see you — to do something for you ! "

"What is there to be done for such a one as I am?" replied Clementine hopelessly.

The words recalled Eugéne to a consciousness of his position. What was there to be done, indeed!

How often he had dreamed of "*La Belle Clementine*" pardoned by the Emperor; how often he had fondly thought he would make her his wife; how often he had pictured their lives in some far-off land, where both would be unknown. But this woman, who, though still strikingly handsome, bore no resemblance to the ideal in his mind — was *she* the being with whom he pined to share the rest of his existence, and for whom no sacrifice could be too great?

"If the Emperor's pardon could be procured — "

He hesitated, and was silent — at a loss how to finish the sentence.

"I have never dared to hope for it!" mournfully ejaculated Clementine.

"But, if it could be obtained, there would be a future still before you!"

"There *is* a future, even here; my life is not wholly useless. I thank God for that."

She could hardly have made a reply that would have touched Eugéne more deeply; there is something so penetrating in the holiness of that resignation which hopes nothing for itself, yet is hopeful and helpful for others. He recognized her voice at last, and it seemed to him more richly melodious than ever.

"*I* will seek for your pardon! To what better object could I devote my life?" he replied, with new ardor.

Clementine's eyes dilated with sudden joy until they seemed a brilliant black; she clasped her hands, and burst into a fit of convulsive weeping.

A jailer entered; the time allowed for the interview had expired. Without being able to utter a single sentence, the convict was compelled to withdraw.

The state in which Eugéne returned to his companion completely puzzled the physician. It was impossible to tell whether his patient was or was not cured, or what effect the great change in Clementine had wrought upon him — he was so excited, yet so eager to leave the island. A very inferior vessel was to sail for France in a few days; its accommodations were of the rudest kind; but Eugéne insisted on taking passage; he could not brook delay; and during the days that intervened before the ship sailed, he made no attempt to see Clementine again.

———

CONCLUSION.

Two years later, the Count was once more on his way to Cayenne; for two years he had labored, first to reach, then to influence those in power, who finally obtained from the Emperor the pardon of which Eugéne was now the bearer. During those two years, no symptom of his mental derangement had been apparent; he had something to achieve, and to a mind in the state of his, occupation is salvation.

Eugéne had made every arrangement for Clementine's instant return to France. His thoughtfulness and delicacy were touchingly evinced in his preparations. He had secured a stateroom on board of the vessel in which he sailed for its return passage, and had provided a trunk containing a fitting wardrobe for a lady.

Did Eugéne remember his frantic impatience to behold Clementine when he entered that port two years before? He betrayed no such eagerness now. He did not even seek the prison. The trunk, with two envelopes addressed to Clementine, were conveyed to her by a trusty messenger. One envelope contained her pardon, the other the ticket for her passage and a handsome sum of money—literally half of all that Eugéne possessed. These gifts she was allowed to believe were part of the Emperor's bounty.

Clementine had gained the respect and esteem of the whole colony, and her departure was the signal for loud lamentations among the poor wretches whose fate her gentle presence and loving ministry had softened. Alas! they were too sorrowful for themselves to be generous enough to rejoice for her.

When the day upon which the vessel was to sail arrived, she was handed on board by the Governor of the island himself. She wore the simplest of the dresses found in the well-filled trunk, but her beauty, so long disguised by the hideous prison garb, shone forth in startling splendor. It was not the beauty of the Clementine of old, but a mellow, subdued, unyouthful, yet heart-touching loveliness. There was not the faintest trace of the twenty years' convict in the dignified gentlewoman with whom the Governor shook hands warmly, as he withdrew, after presenting her to the captain of the vessel. The captain himself conducted her to her stateroom.

As she was walking by his side, she started violently, and left a sentence unfinished. She had caught sight of some one in the distance, who lifted his hat. Eugéne, as he advanced to greet her, experienced a sense of inexplicable gratification when he found her so powerfully agitated, that, after stammering out a few inarticulate words, she retired to her stateroom, and did not re-appear until the vessel had sailed.

It was a moonlight evening. Eugéne was pacing the deck, in so happy a frame of mind, that he wondered at himself, when he again beheld "*La Belle Clementine*"—he had once more involuntarily restored to her the familiar name by which, during the last two years, he had ceased to designate her in thought.

She came towards him as rapidly as the motion of the vessel would permit, with an air of mingled timidity and frankness. He hastened to offer his arm; she hesitated—but the lurching of the vessel per force overcame her unwillingness to accept its support.

"I came to thank you—no, not to thank you—that is impossible; you have given me life itself, and all the thanks I could utter—"

Eugéne interrupted her—"would but pain me. Do not thank me for purchasing the greatest happiness that was ever mine by an act which is one of simple justice to you."

The eyes which Clementine lifted to his face looked wondrously blue in the moonlight; womanly instinct taught her that he would accept their thanks, while he refused those of her lips.

The passage was long, for the ship was often becalmed, but the days were all too short for Eugéne. He loved "*La Belle Clementine*" as fervently as ever; or rather, he now loved the true Clementine, whose mind and heart were daily revealed to him, not the creature of his imagination, to whom she bore so little resemblance.

And Clementine, how was it with her? Alas! how alone could it be? Her early passion for Victorien had been as mad as Eugéne's infatuation for her former self, and, like his, was the mere idolatry of an ideal; but this man, who had loved her so many years ; this man, who had brought the light of hope, beaming from his face, into her prison house — who had broken her chains, restored her to life — was it wonderful that in his presence she walked in paradise?

But in the heart of a true woman love is indissolubly united to boundless generosity. And when Eugéne asked Clementine to be his wife, though her frame thrilled with joy as her ears drank in the delicious words, she did not betray by the quivering of a muscle her internal ecstacy. She had long known that his noble and generous nature would not let him shrink from offering her the safe shelter of his heart, the shield of his name, and she had pondered well over her course.

In reply to his prayer, she calmly pictured to him what his future life would inevitably be *if* she had returned his affection — (*if?* oh, holy hypocrite!) — *if* she had consented to become his wife; and she painted what her own misery would have been when she felt him dragged down and shut out from fellowship with his equals, by his union with a pardoned convict — greater misery, she added, vehemently, than she had endured at Cayenne — aye, far greater!

The Count de Rosier, she said, had still a career of honor and usefulness before him; he could never sink back into the gloom which, through an imaginary passion for her, and a too absorbing sympathy with her misfortunes, had darkened his past life. The very memory of the benefits he had conferred upon her *must* brighten the rest of his existence.

As for herself, the good old priest at Cayenne had given her a letter to a holy father in Paris. She had made up her mind to take such vows as the law permitted, and become a Sister of Charity. She chose this vocation of her own free will, for the Emperor's pardon had been accompanied by a gift which secured her independence. She had placed half the sum in the hands of her friend, the priest, at Cayenne, to be used in ameliorating the condition of the convicts; the other half would go to the Order of Sisters which she joined.

Certes it was not for these purposes that Eugéne had impoverished himself by diminishing. his own moderate income to half, but there was nothing to be done.

Again and again he pressed his suit — ever with the same result. Clementine preserved her secret with such womanly art, that Eugéne at last believed her true to the villain who had caused her ruin, and was compelled to abandon all hope.

When they parted at the door of the priest to whom she had been recommended, Eugéne uttered one more remonstrance, but this time only against her becoming a Sister of Charity. The door had just opened to admit her; for the first time she laid her hand in his; then, with a smile that seemed to glorify her face, said, "Be sure it was for that I was made!" and passed from his sight.

And soon there were sufferers not a few, whose grateful voices testified to the truth of these words, proclaiming that she had indeed God's license to minister.

Eugéne had no mental relapse. IIis cure was effected in a manner somewhat different from the one which Dr. Blanche had planned; but it was complete, and all the more permanent because the bestowal of half his fortune upon Clementine forced him to seek some bread-yielding occupation.

Now and then, as he passes through the streets of Paris, he encounters a Madonna-faced woman, wearing the white coif, serge dress, and large white collar of the Sisterhood of Charity; and though her meek gray eyes are never raised to any other face, recognition of a male not being permitted to her order, she smiles upon him with grave sweetness, and the smile seems to say,—

"What should I have been but for you?"

Eugéne cannot doubt that she is happy, and her existence of helpful charity, of self-abnegation, and peaceful satisfaction, has taught him the wisdom of angels who know that,—

> "From deepest woe divinest joy proceeds;
> No human heart, until it inly bleeds
> Its life away in pure self-sacrifice,
> Can teach to earth the wisdom of the skies."

CATERINA SFORZA.

THRICE WEDDED, THRICE WIDOWED.
An Italian Châtelaine.

PART I.

THERE is a State Prison in Florence called the *Muraté*, which but a few years ago was the old *Muraté* convent, inhabited exclusively by noble ladies, who, in weary disgust or penitential sorrow, had retired from the storms or allurements of the world. In that convent died Caterina Sforza — one of the most lion-hearted, indomitable, yet fascinating and beautiful women of her age; an impressive type of the Italian *châtelaine* of the fifteenth century.

Caterina's life was replete with those startling incidents and sudden changes which give to history the high coloring of a sensational romance. She was the illegitimate daughter of Galeazzo Maria Sforza, Duke of Milan, and was born 1462. When she had reached her eighth year, the Duke caused her to be "*legitimatized*," and his gentle second wife, the Duchess Bona, soon after her marriage, affectionately received the precocious child into her princely home, and did not cease tenderly to watch over the little stranger when she herself became a mother, nor to give her the precedence due to the eldest daughter of the noble house of Sforza.

It is related of Duke Galeazzo, whose court was renowned for its luxury, vice, and splendor, that, having exhausted all amusements in turn, he found his highest enjoyment in witnessing tortures, executions, and cruel mutilations. The sight of death and human decay excited in him such ferocious delight, that he even frequented charnel-houses, and caused graves to be torn open that he might gaze upon corruption.

When Caterina was eleven years years of age she was publicly betrothed, by proxy, to Girolamo Riario, a nephew of Pope Sixtus IV.

"The great Galeazzo," the "*superb Duke*," lived but thirty-two years to blot the annals of history with the record of his unsurpassed abominations. In December of the year 1476, three youths, one of whom came to avenge a sister whom the Duke had brought to shame, waited for their sovereign at the door of the Cathedral of St. Stephen's, and although the Duke was surrounded by his guards, stabbed him mortally.

In May, 1477, Caterina was married, by proxy, at Milan, to Girolamo Riario, whom she had not yet seen. The recent death of the Duke forbade all festivities, and the youthful bride departed immediately to join her bridegroom at Rome. She had smiled upon only fifteen birthdays when, accompanied by her bridegroom, and mounted upon a richly caparisoned steed, she rode through the *Porta del Popolo* into Rome. She was eminently beautiful and superbly attired, and, as she passed through the *Piazza of the famed old Pantheon,* in the midst of a brilliant cavalcade, to the magnificent residence of her husband, on the banks of the Tiber, all Rome grew wild with enthusiastic admiration.

The *Palazzo Corsini* now rears its noble walls where the Riario palace then stood.

Caterina's influence soon became all-powerful with Pope Sixtus and his court; it is said the princes of Italy who had any favors to ask of the Apostolic See had only to secure her intercession to obtain their wishes.

Shortly after his bridal, Girolamo, with much ceremony, was made a citizen of Rome. Later, he received from the Pope investiture of the city and county of *Forli,* one of the most important towns of

The Pantheon and Egyptian Obelisk in the Piazza Rotunda, at Rome.—
Page 270.

Romagna, and near the principality of *Imola*, brought to him by his wife. He was also made generalissimo·of the Papal forces.

On Easter Day, the 26th of April, 1478, *Lorenzo de Medici*, called the "Magnificent," and his brother Giuliano, were stabbed by assassins in the cathedral at Florence — Giuliano, mortally; Lorenzo not fatally. Florentine historians declare that Girolamo was one of the conspirators who planned the infamous deed, and one writer adds, " These things were ordered by Pope Sixtus, to take away the dominion of Florence from *Lorenzo de Medici*, and give it to Count Girolamo."

It was well known that Girolamo, who had the highest appreciation of *Caterina's* superior intellect, consulted her upon all state affairs; but that he made her the *confidante* of this murderous project seems improbable. She was but sixteen, and about to become a mother; there is no proof that she had any knowledge of her husband's crime.

The first infant to whom she gave birth was a daughter, Bianca, whose sex occasioned her parents severe and undisguised disappointment — a disappointment, however, which was not repeated, for Caterina never bore another daughter, though she gave birth to numerous sons. To no woman could have been more appropriately applied Shakespeare's adjuration,

> "Bring forth men children only,
> For thy undaunted mettle should compose
> Nothing but males!"

The next year a son, Ottaviano, was born, and a second son the succeeding year.

After passing four years in Rome, Girolamo and his young wife, for the first time, visited their dominions of Forli and Imola. The journey occupied eight days, and the *cortége* of the youthful couple resembled a triumphal procession, terminating with a train of horses in rich housings, mules bearing heavy loads or drawing well-filled carts, and each mule-load covered with an embroidered cloth, showing the arms of Rovere and Sforza, and bound with silken cords, and each cart similarly protected.

The citizens of Forli hailed with exuberant demonstrations of joy the entrance of all this wealth into their city. Young men, and maidens dressed in white, and bearing olive-branches in their hands, preceded by the clergy and magistrates in their robes of office, went out to welcome their sovereigns. The Count and Countess descended from their horses and received them standing. Every one was charmed by the beauty of Caterina, who wore her most gorgeous gala dress, and her costliest pearls and diamonds. The homage of the city was offered in a very choice oration, and in replying, the Count was pleased to remit the corn duties, which gave great satisfaction.

For three days there were public rejoicings throughout Forli. In the principal square a tournament was held, in which the Roman princes joined. A vast wooden castle was constructed in the middle of the piazza, and besieged and defended by two parties of the town-people. A reward was given to the first of the besieging party who entered. Unfortunately it cost the youth who accomplished the feat an eye.

Then there was a grand ball, at which the Count and Countess led the dance, and, says the historian, "there were, of course, triumphal arches, allegorical paintings, cunning carpentry, devices moving by unseen means; eating, drinking, and speechifying, in prose and verse, to a wonderful extent. And charming it was to see the lady Countess and all her damsels come forth in different magnificent dresses every day for a whole week, and the great buffets, ten feet high, in the banqueting-hall of the palace, loaded every day with a fresh service of silver and gold."

Far different was the scene that palace was to witness when a few years had swept on !

12*

The youthful couple, after they had sojourned in
Forli nearly a month, visited Imola, where the festive welcome was repeated in a more moderate
manner.

The Count occupied himself in the improvement
of both cities; schools were established, palaces
enlarged, public squares adorned, streets paved,
and an academy of fine arts instituted.

The first visit of the Count and Caterina to Imola
was but short.   After a sojourn of three weeks they
left for Venice, to carry out certain ambitious views
of the Pope.   It is expressly stated that Caterina
accompanied her husband because he so thoroughly
relied upon her counsel and judgment.   He was
not, however, successful in his mission, though
Venice received the noble guests with unstinted
pomp and multiplied festivities in their honor.

Shortly after the return of the Count and Countess to Imola, they received news from Tolentino,
the trusty Governor of Forli, of a conspiracy which
had for its object the restoration of the dynasty of the
Ordelaffi, the ancient masters of Forli, from whom
it had been unrighteously wrested by the Pope.
The conspirators had agreed to assassinate Girolamo
on his journey from Imola to Forli.   The Count and
Countess hastened to Forli on hearing these tidings,
for the danger was over, and after a brief stay there,

returned to Rome. On the tenth day following their departure, the four corpses of the conspirators were seen dangling from the windows of the Palazzo Pubblico.

Girolamo was now called upon to head the Papal troops, and to give battle to the Neapolitans near Velletri. In company with Robert Malatesta, who commanded the Venetians, he won a great victory, marched in triumph back to Rome, and presented the banners, taken in battle, to his exulting Countess.

Robert Malatesta died of fever soon after the conquest he had gained, and his death was attributed to poison administered by Girolamo out of military jealousy.

Rome had begun to be the scene of great distress and discontent. There was a scarcity of grain, of wine, and provisions; and the deadly feud between the implacable *Colonna* and the furious *Orsini,* kept the Eternal City in a constant state of anarchy. The Pope and Girolamo warmly espoused the cause of the Orsini. In March, 1484, all the *Orsini* headed by Girolamo, armed themselves, and attacked one of the palaces of the Colonna. A fearful tumult was the sequence: the houses not only of the Colonna, but of many private citizens, were sacked, and all manner of atrocities committed.

In the midst of these disturbances Pope Sixtus

died, on the 12th of August, 1484; and great was the change for Caterina and Girolamo, whom Rome now hated. Caterina was alone, for Girolamo was driving the Colonna out of their fortresses in the neighborhood of the city. She was a woman of great energy, and prompt in her decisions; she saw her danger, and immediately took possession of the Castle of St. Angelo, in the name of her husband, as commander of the forces, and during the first outburst of anarchy that followed the Pontiff's death, she and her children were safe.

Girolamo returned to Rome, to find his palace utterly devastated. Even the marble doorways and window-cases were wrenched off and carried away, and the gardens and green-houses torn and trampled into ruins. Girolamo deemed it wise to leave Rome with his wife and children. They arrived at Forli on the 4th of September. How different had been their entrance into that city only a few short years before! Where, now, was the festive welcome? Where, now, were the olive branches and rejoicings, the ball and tournament? They were met in silence.

During the next four years evil auguries multiplied. Girolamo needed money, and re-imposed the taxes he had taken off; this, and his other well-known misdeeds, daily increased his unpopularity, and rendered his position perilous.

Caterina became the mother of three more sons during those four years.

An event of great importance marked this fourth year. Tolentino, the faithful Governor of Forli, who once warned Girolamo of the conspiracy against him, had died, and one Melchior Zocchejo, of Savona, a ferocious and worthless man, had been appointed *Castellano* of *Ravaldino*, the magnificent fortress built at Forli, by Girolamo. Codronchi, the seneschal of the palace, who had formed an intimacy with Zocchejo, managed one night to introduce several bravoes, in the guise of servants, into the fort, killed Zocchejo, and became master of the fortress. It was supposed the Codronchi had been won over by the Ordelaffi, and that the fortress and the city were lost to the Count and Countess. When a messenger reached Imola with these terrible tidings, the Count was too ill to travel, and Caterina was daily expecting her fifth confinement; yet, prompt and undismayed as ever, she mounted her horse, and by midnight was before the gate of the Ravaldino, calling upon Codronchi to account for his conduct.

The seneschal appeared upon the battlements, and entreated the lady to seek repose, and return in the

morning and breakfast at the fort, as he could say
no more that night.

Caterina had no alternative but to accept the in-
vitation, and withdraw. The next morning she re-
appeared before the walls, with attendants bearing
provisions for an excellent breakfast. She was told
that no one but herself and one servant to carry the
breakfast would be admitted. The brave Caterina
reflected a few moments; if the man *had* been
bought over by the *Ordelaffi*, if she trusted herself
within those walls, her fate was sealed; but what
could she accomplish if she did not run the risk?
Her counsellors strongly advised her to refuse to
enter, but she boldly passed in with the groom who
bore the provisions.

After a brief stay she came forth, and sent for
Tommaso Feo, one of her most highly esteemed
friends, and returned into the fortress with him.
Codronchi gave over the command into his hands.
Feo was left as *Castellano*, and Caterina, with Codronchi, proceeded to the Palazzo Pubblico, where a
great crowd had assembled.

The Countess addressed the citizens in these
words: "Know, my men of Forli, that Ravaldino
was lost to me and to the city, by the means of this
Innocenzio Codronchi here; but I have recovered it,
and have left it in right trusty hands!"

The seneschal confessed himself a traitor, by re-marking that "it was true enough!"

What persuasions Caterina employed to induce him to yield up the fortress, are not recorded; but it was saved by her voice only.

On leaving the Palazzo Pubblico, the Countess and Codronchi mounted their horses and rode to Imola. The next morning Caterina gave birth to a son.

Girolamo soon recovered, and returned with Caterina to Forli. Shortly after his arrival, one evening, at his usual hour of receiving guests, he was leaning out of a window of his palace when he was sudden-ly stabbed by one of the *Orsi* family. At this time Caterina was twenty-six years of age, and had six children.

PART II.

The news of her husband's murder was carried to Caterina by an affrighted servant. In spite of the horror and consternation of the moment, Caterina, as usual, did not lose her presence of mind. She sent the man in all haste to tell Feo, the governor of the fort, whom she had installed in the summary manner we have described, to send couriers to her brother, the Duke of Milan, and to the Lord of Bologna. Then she barricaded herself in her chamber, with her women, her children, and her young sister Stella. But the assassin of Girolamo, with half a dozen ruffians, attacked the door, broke through the barricade, and led the Countess and her children captive through the crowded streets to the palace of the Orsi, who had ever been her bitterest foes, and were now her husband's murderers.

The body of the hated tyrant had been thrown from the window into the *piazza*, and the mob tore off the clothing and dragged the corpse naked through the streets, until some pitying friars got possession of the mangled remains, and carried them into the sacristy of their church.

Cardinal Savelli, who was leagued with the conspirators, visited Caterina, and suggested that she and her family would be safer in a small but strong building over St. Peter's gateway. Caterina unhesitatingly agreed to the change, preferring any prison to the palace of her husband's destroyer.

That night, the 15th of April, a troop of soldiers bearing torches marched the beautiful and haughty Countess, her mother, her sister Stella, her six children, two nurses, and a natural son of her husband, through the streets to her new prison; and here they were all confined together, in an exceedingly small room.

It is worthy of note, that Caterina, herself an illegitimate child, who had been tenderly nurtured by her father's wife, had been mindful to repay the debt by her care of her husband's illegitimate offspring.

On the day following Caterina's removal to prison, Cardinal Savelli and the conspirators ordered Feo, the Governor of Ravaldino, to deliver up the fortress. Feo, of course, refused. Then Caterina was conducted to the foot of the walls, and compelled to order the *Castellano* to yield the fort, that he might thus save her life. The Governor looking down upon her from the ramparts, and thoroughly comprehending, from his knowledge of her character, what her real wishes must be, remained firm in his refusal.

Caterina was led back to prison, and that night the faithful servant who had brought her the news of her husband's death, and had carried her message to the Governor of the fortress, secretly gained admission to her. She bade him tell Feo to hold out hope of yielding the fortress, when the demand was again made, but to stipulate that she should first enter alone, that they might converse freely. This same trusty servant, acting on Caterina's suggestion, also saw the Cardinal, and dexterously hinted that the surest mode of inducing Feo to yield was to allow him to have a private interview with the Countess.

The next day, Caterina, as she had anticipated, was again taken to the fortress, and the Cardinal himself proposed to Feo that she should be allowed to enter, asking if he would obey her orders if he found she was not acting upon compulsion. Feo cautiously replied, that, after conversing with his mistress, he would do whatever seemed to him his duty.

Caterina was allowed to enter unattended, with the understanding that she was to come forth in three hours. During those hours a noisy and impatient multitude waited in front of the ramparts.

The great bell of the *piazza* told that the three hours had expired; the murmuring voices sank to silence, all was hushed expectation, when, in obedience to the summons of a trumpet, Feo appeared upon the battlements.

With the utmost *sang froid* he informed the eager crowd that his lady was much fatigued; that as soon as she entered the fort, he had compelled her to seek repose; that she was now asleep, and he did not choose to disturb her; that when she awoke, he did not intend to permit her to go forth, as he judged that she was safer in the fortress.

Having spoken these words, he withdrew.

The crowd became furious; the Cardinal saw that he had been duped. The Orsi rushed to the prison, seized Caterina's children, hurried them to the walls of the fortress, summoned the *Castellano*, and bade him tell his mistress that their lives depended upon her keeping her promise.

Feo replied in the most imperturbable manner, that he would carry no such message; and he warned the citizens of Forli to reflect upon the inevitable consequences to themselves if they suffered those children, the nephews of the Duke of Milan, and protected by the Lord of Bologna, to receive the slightest injury.

The enraged and baffled Orsi, the Cardinal, and the citizens knew too well how much reason there was in this menace; and the children were carried back to their prison unharmed.

But the father of the Orsi, a veteran of eighty-five years, who had been engaged in seven insurrections, severely rebuked his sons for sparing the children, and warned them that they had committed a fatal error in allowing Caterina to enter an impregnable fortress. By his advice they at once despatched messengers to Rome, to lay the obedience of the city at the feet of the Pontiff, and urge him to send troops and munitions for their defence.

Meantime, on the 17th, the fort was attacked, and Feo in return bombarded the city.

On the 18th, a herald from the Lord of Bologna arrived in Forli, and made proclamation that the city would be entirely destroyed if any harm was done to the children of the Count, and demanded that Caterina should be set at liberty, and her eldest son Ottaviano proclaimed Count of Forli.

Cardinal Savelli gave answer to the herald, that the Countess was already at liberty, that her children were safe, but that Ottaviano could not be proclaimed Count of Forli, as an embassy had been sent to Rome to lay the fealty of the city at the feet of the Pope.

On the 20th came letters from the Duke of Milan, one reproving the Cardinal Savelli, and one ordering the citizens to send away the Cardinal and return to their allegiance, or abide the consequences of a refusal.

The next day, two heralds, one from the Duke of Milan and one from the Lord of Bologna, rode into the great square of Forli, and demanded the children of the Count.

Checco d'Orsi, who slew their father, insolently replied that the children had already been put to death, and that Forli feared neither the Duke of Milan, nor the Lord of Bologna, as the Pope's troops

would be within the gates before the Milanese could
reach the city.

Pope Innocent VIII., however, had no intention
of taking part in the fray, and though Cardinal Savelli forged a letter from the Pope, promising
speedily to send troops, its authenticity was gener-
ally doubted.

Savelli continued to attack the citadel with cannon, and Feo continued to batter the city from his
ramparts, until, on the 29th, the armies of the Duke
of Milan and the Bolognese were before the walls
of Forli. At this crisis, papers signed by Caterina
were scattered about the streets, soon after dark,
entreating her loyal subjects to put to death the
conspirators, and promising rewards to every man
whose dagger was thus employed.

The Orsi tried to obtain, by stratagem, possession
of Caterina's children, but failed, and fled from the
city on the 30th of April.

If Caterina had acted in accordance with the custom of those days, she would have given Forli up to
be sacked by the soldiers who had come to her rescue; but she saved her subjects from this chastisement, and announced to them that they were spared
for the sake of the women of Forli, though the
men had not deserved mercy at her hands.

The magistrates went in procession to Caterina

in the fortress, and delivered to her the key of the city. She made a triumphal entrance on horseback, between the generals of the forces sent to support her.

It is easy to conceive the affecting meeting between Caterina and her children. Ottaviano, nine years of age, was proclaimed Count and his mother made "Regent," and the murdered Girolamo was buried with great pomp at Imola.

Caterina's sister Stella, who was betrothed to one Andrea Ricci, had, some time before this, found means to leave the Gatehouse prison and hasten to his bedside; for he was lying ill of the wounds he had received in the general fight that occurred immediately after Girolamo was murdered. She was hastily united to her wounded lover, and then permitted to depart with her mother to Cesena.

Clemency was not esteemed a virtue in those days, and Caterina was far more merciful than the code of her age justified. Only a few who had taken part in the conspiracy were executed; among them the man who threw the Count's body out of the window, and the veteran *Orsi*, whose great age caused him to be left behind when his children fled.

His chastisement was terrible. Before he was executed, he was brought forth, his long silver locks flowing on his shoulders, his hands bound behind his back, a halter about his neck, and conducted by the hangman through the streets, and placed in front of his ancestral home, which was razed to the ground before his eyes. Having witnessed that sight, far more terrible to him than death itself, the old patrician was led, by the halter, back to the *piazza* and bound upon a stout plank, which was attached to the tail of a powerful horse. The feet of the prisoner were nearest to the horse; the head, passing beyond the length of the board, fell back upon the stones: in this manner he was dragged twice around the *piazza*, and before he was quite dead, his side was opened, and his heart torn out and rent to pieces before the people.

Caterina was a young and exceedingly beautiful widow, and the aspirants to her hand were not few. She was a woman to choose according to the dictates of her heart, but her maternal instincts were too strong for her to imperil the interests of her children.

Feo, the faithful governor of the citadel, had a brother not yet twenty years of age, a remarkably handsome youth, who is described as "well skilled in all manly and noble exercises." Feo had married a relative of the Countess, and after this union the brothers were freely admitted into the society of the Countess.

That Caterina very soon became enamored of this
young and captivating Giacomo Feo, there can be
no doubt, and she conceived the idea of giving him
his brother's place as Governor of Ravaldino. But
how was this to be accomplished? She could
hardly dismiss Tommasso Feo, who had obeyed her
orders so faithfully, and to whose allegiance she
owed, perhaps, her life. It is even suggested by
historians, that as it is a good *castellano's* duty to
hold his castle at all hazards, it would not have
been an easy matter to displace Tommasso Feo, by
ordering him to give up his command.

Caterina, as we have seen, had an abundance of
woman's wit at her command, to effect any object
upon which she had set her heart. She gave a
splendid *fête* in her gardens outside of the city, and
invited her *castellano*. Throughout the day she
leaned upon his arm, and toward evening requested
him to escort her through the little city to her
palace; thus taking him captive, while he was
unsuspicious, and only flattered by the distinction.
Once within the palace walls, he was politely desired to yield up his sword, and informed that he
was a prisoner. He saw at once that he had been
caught in a trap, and made no resistance.

Giacomo was then summoned, and the Countess
informed him that, although she had the highest

confidence in his brother, she had found it desirable for Tommasso to visit his native Savona, and that Giacomo was to fill his vacant post, and become governor of the fort.

There is reason to suppose that, at this very time, Giacomo had for some months been married to the Countess. Although the union was perfectly legal, it was kept secret, because Caterina would cease to be the guardian of her children, if it could be proved that she had contracted a second marriage.

A few months after the new governor was installed, Caterina gave birth to a son, who was named *Giacomo*.

PART III.

Caterina delighted in showering favors upon her young husband. She obtained for him, from the Duke of Milan, an order of chivalry. All the customary insignia were sent by heralds from that sumptuous court. Great were the festive rejoicings, and the devoted wife took care that Giacomo should be invested with the cloak, collar, and spurs, by the noblest knights of the highest families in Forli.

Her marriage did not render her a less exemplary

mother; she still personally superintended the education of her children, and took untiring pains to promote their welfare.

Pope Innocent VIII. died, and Cardinal Roderigo Borgia succeeded him as Pope Alexander VI. History testifies that the life of this pontiff was a series of the most detestable and open crimes. A strong friendship had existed between Cardinal Borgia and Caterina's first husband, and when the Cardinal was elected to the papal throne, she thought it politic to despatch two envoys in behalf of Forli and two in behalf of Imola to compliment the Pope on his election, and offer the homage of both cities.

A few years later, in the summer of 1494, Charles VII. of France laid claim to the sovereignty of Naples, and marched into Italy. Forli was in a dangerous position between the Neapolitan troops at Cesena and the French troops at Bologna; and Caterina was forced to side with one party or the other. After more than usual hesitation, for promptness of decision was her especial characteristic, she declared herself the ally of the king of Naples, on condition that Rome and Naples agreed to defend her states, and that her son, Ottaviano, now seventeen years old, received the rank of general in the allied army, with a large stipend. The

French, however, met with unexpected successes.
Forli was not protected as stipulated, and Caterina
deliberately changed sides and made friends with
the victors.

During this period the young Giacomo Feo had
acted as governor-general of Caterina's states; and
she finally obtained for him from the King of
France the rank and title of general. It is recorded that Giacomo was highly elated by this distinction; but alas! his promotion proved a fatal
boon: it awakened the jealousy of the citizens of
Imola and Forli, and seven of them took a vow
that they would kill the pampered favorite.

On the 27th of August, 1495, Giacomo went
hunting with Caterina and her sons. When the
party returned in the evening, Caterina and some of
her children were in a carriage, behind which came
Feo on horseback. The seven conspirators had
grouped themselves just within the city walls, for
they had sworn to fulfil their oaths that day. After
Caterina and her sons had passed, they suddenly
rushed upon the newly made general; a pike
pierced his body, he uttered but one cry, and fell
dead! Caterina, affrighted by the shrieks of some
of her retainers, looked back, and saw her husband
slain, and her attendants flying in all directions.

She and her sons hastily mounted horses taken from the grooms, and galloped to the fortress.

At the age of thirty-three, the heroic *châtelaine* was for the *second time a widow, and again the widow of a murdered husband!*

There was a strong manifestation of popular indignation in Forli against the assassins. That night they were hunted through the town, and the next morning carried to the *piazza*, where some were quartered alive, some dragged by horses through the streets.

In those days, in Italy, the whole male portion of the family of a political conspirator was included in his condemnation; but the vengeance of Caterina was not limited to *sex*. Even the women, children, and babes of the guilty men were brutally slaughtered at her command; not one babe was spared! She had never before evinced such a degree of savage, pitiless cruelty, though its exercise was entirely in accordance with the creed of her time. Between forty and fifty persons were put to death to avenge the murder of Giacomo; and while the bodies of the criminals were hanging from the windows of the *Palazzo Pubblico*, Feo was buried with even greater pomp than his murdered predecessor, Girolamo.

Caterina's temperament was too elastic and her

mind too vigorous for even grief to render it inactive. She found in incessant occupation a balm for her sorrow. During the first two years of her widowhood she sought distraction by tearing down the palace at Forli, to which such odious associations were attached, and building one more magnificent, near to the fortress Ravaldino. She purchased a large tract of land adjoining the new palace, and cultivated orchards, and dairy pastures, and beautiful gardens and pleasure grounds, and hunting grounds, until the only fitting name for the rural Elysium with which she had encompassed herself was pronounced to be "The Paradise."

In the third year of her widowhood, Caterina formed a third alliance — from motives of policy and ambition, it is supposed, rather than of affection. Again she chose a husband younger than herself. She was then thirty-five, and her third bridegroom, Giovanni de Medici, ambassador from the Republic of Florence to Forli, and great grandson of that *Giovanni* who was the founder of the *Medicean* greatness, was but thirty. Caterina's third husband, though he fought bravely under Charles VIII. of France, and was a wise statesman, holds no conspicuous place in history.

Her nuptials were again kept secret, for the same

reason which had before rendered concealment imperative.

The offspring of this union was the only one of
Caterina's children who became renowned. The
son to whom she gave birth in the first year of this
marriage became that celebrated *Giovanni Delle
Bande Neré*, who was looked upon as the greatest
captain of his day, and from whom descended the
long line of Tuscan Grand Dukes of the Medicean
race. He was Caterina's eighth child and seventh
son.

Caterina's third husband was in delicate health at
the time of their union, and he died six months
after the birth of his son, in the second year of his
marriage.

Pope Alexander, in spite of the "homage" paid
him by Caterina, when he was called to the Papal
throne, soon manifested unfriendly intentions.
This unscrupulous Borgia had sons, whom he did
not even pretend (according to the custom of Popes)
were his *nephews*. To enrich these sons was his
first care, and under various pretexts he declared
sundry little potentates of Romagna deposed from
their sovereignties, and Caterina among them. But,
with her wonted bravery, she defied the Pope himself, and determined "to preserve her son's sceptre

for him as long as the walls of the city and fortress
would hold together."

Louis XII. (who succeeded Charles VIII.) entered
into a league with Pope Alexander, and undertook
to seize the Duchy of Milan; while Cesare Borgia,
the Pope's eldest son, took possession of Imola and
Forli, and other principalities of Romagna. Borgia
appeared with his army before the walls of Imola;
the city was quickly forced to surrender, but not so
the Castellano of the fortress, who made answer
that he would only yield when the fort was in ruins.

Caterina and her son Ottaviano were preparing
to defend Forli. She personally superintended the
repairing of the fortifications, and Ottaviano labored
with his own hands. But the citizens of Forli
showed but little inclination to resist the Borgia;
and Caterina retired into the citadel with her personal adherents, first sending Ottaviano to Tuscany,
to secure his personal safety. When she found all
her efforts to rouse the city in vain, the resolute
châtelaine opened the guns of her fortress upon
Forli, as a punishment for the desertion of her vas-
sals.

On the 19th of December, 1499, Cesare Borgia
marched into Forli. T. A. Trollope says of this
triumphal entry, " The troops and their officers having filed into the city before him, the great man —

most wicked, base, and incapable of any great or
noble thought, of all men there; the great man
most reverenced, admired, obeyed of all men there,
— advanced stately, in full armor, on a white horse,
with a heraldically embroidered silk tunic over his
armor, a tall white plume nodding above his hel-
met, and in his hand a long green lance, the point of
which rested on the toe of his boot."

But a sudden storm dispersed the procession, and
the soldiers rushed about the city, finding lodgings
wherever they chose — turning the Council-hall into
a tavern, making themselves masters alike of the
public palace and private residences, and to all in-
tents and purposes sacking the city into which they
had been admitted as friends; thus the citizens
were most unexpectedly and *doubly* chastised for
not rallying around their liege lady.

Borgia, after having twice parleyed with Caterina,
attacked the fortress towards the end of December.
For a week she defended herself ably; then a truce
of a few days was agreed upon, and the attack was
renewed on the 10th of January. At mid-day on
the 12th, a breach was nearly practicable, and later
on the same day a fire broke out in the fort, which
paralyzed the garrison, and the principal part of the
fortifications fell into the hands of the enemy. But
the undaunted Caterina retired into the principal

tower, and held her ground. A large number of
the enemy had penetrated into another tower, which
served a magazine, and there met a terrible fate;
for it was fired by Caterina's people, though apparently not by her order.

Borgia again demanded parley, and Caterina appeared at the window of her tower; but while she
was standing there, reiterating her refusal to yield,
a French soldier, who had found some means of access to the tower, came behind her, and made her
prisoner, in the name of the General.

That night Borgia and the French General visited
the haughty lady in her citadel, and it is recorded
that during the interview "the sounds of falling
masonry and exploding mines, the shouts of the pur-
suers, and the cries of the conquered as they fell,
ever and anon came through the thick walls, and
gave clear evidence of the work of destruction which
was in progress."

Towards the close of January, Borgia returned to
Rome with his noble captive.

Caterina, arrayed in a black satin dress, made the
journey on horseback, riding between Borgia and
a French General. Once more she entered
Rome; through that Porta del Popolo, which she
had first passed in triumphal procession, clothed in
bridal robes, a joyous and beautiful bride of sixteen,

welcomed by the whole city, she now rode, conquered and despoiled, robed in black, *thrice wedded
and thrice widowed*, with a victorious foe on either
side of her rudely uncaparisoned steed ! She was
led to the Vatican, which in those unforgotten days
had so often been filled with cringing courtiers, too
happy to receive a smile or a word from the Pope's
favorite — now to be stared at, pitied, or disdained
as a Pope's prisoner.

An apartment in the *Belvidere* of the Vatican
was made her place of confinement. Four months
later she was accused of having attempted the life
of the Pope, by endeavoring to send him letters rendered contagious by being placed upon the breast of
one who was dying of the plague. Although this
accusation could not be supported, it was rendered
the pretext for transferring her from the *Belvidere*
to the dungeons of the Castle of St. Angelo, where it
was no doubt intended that she should find a living
tomb.

She owed her life to the interposition and remon-
strances of Louis XII. As she had been captured by
one of his Generals, his voice could not remain un-
heeded by the Pope. After only four days' incar-
ceration she was liberated, at the French King's request, and allowed to travel unmolested to Florence,
where all her children had found a refuge.

She was only thirty-nine years of age; but into those thirty-nine years what a multitude of thrilling events had been crowded! She was wearied out, crushed, spirit-conquered at last; she had done with life — the life of the world; even the presence of her children could no longer render that outer world endurable. She at once retired to the Convent of the *Murate*, and never again passed its walls.

She died in 1509, in the forty-seventh year of her age, and was buried in the chapel of the convent, where her monument was visible until a few years ago, when the convent was converted into a State-prison.

"Non v' ha cosa infinità qué guí."

THE END.

Mrs. Mary J. Holmes' Works.

'LENA RIVERS.—	A novel	12mo. cloth,	$1.50
DARKNESS AND DAYLIGHT.—	do.	do.	$1.50
TEMPEST AND SUNSHINE.—	do.	do.	$1.50
MARIAN GREY.—	do.	do.	$1.50
MEADOW BROOK.—	do.	do.	$1 50
ENGLISH ORPHANS.—	do.	do.	$1.50
DORA DEANE.—	do.	do.	$1.50
COUSIN MAUDE.—	do.	do.	$1.50
HOMESTEAD ON THE HILLSIDE.—	do.	do.	$1.50
HUGH WORTHINGTON.—	do.	do.	$1.50
THE CAMERON PRIDE.—	do.	do.	$1.50
ROSE MATHER.—	do.	do.	$1.50
ETHELYN'S MISTAKE.—*Just Published.* do.	do.	$1.50

Miss Augusta J. Evans.

BEULAH.—A novel of great power.	12mo. cloth,	$1.75
MACARIA.— do. do.	do.	$1.75
ST. ELMO.— do. do.	do.	$2.00
VASHTI.— do. do. *Just Published.* do	$2.00

Victor Hugo.

LES MISÉRABLES.—The celebrated novel.   One large 8vo volume, paper covers, $2.00 ;   .   .   .   cloth bound, $2.50

LES MISÉRABLES.—Spanish. Two vols.. paper, $4.00 ; cl., $5.00

Mrs. A. P. Hill.

MRS. HILL'S NEW COOKERY BOOK, and receipts.   .   .$2.00

Algernon Charles Swinburne.

LAUS VENERIS, AND OTHER POEMS.—   .   12mo. cloth, $1.75

Captain Mayne Reid's Works—Illustrated.

THE SCALP HUNTERS.—	A romance.	12mo. cloth,	$1.50
THE RIFLE RANGERS.—	do.	do.	$1.50
THE TIGER HUNTER.—	do.	do.	$1.50
OSCEOLA, THE SEMINOLE.—	do.	do.	$1.50
THE WAR TRAIL.—	do.	do	$1.50
THE HUNTER'S FEAST.—	do.	do.	$1.50
RANGERS AND REGULATORS.—	do.	do.	$1.50
THE WHITE CHIEF.—	do.	do.	$1.50
THE QUADROON.—	do.	do.	$1.50
THE WILD HUNTRESS.—	do	do.	$1.50
THE WOOD RANGERS.—	do.	do.	$1 50
WILD LIFE.—	do.	do.	$1 50
THE MAROON.—	do.	do.	$1.50
LOST LEONORE.—	do.	do.	$1.50
THE HEADLESS HORSEMAN.—	do.	do.	$1.50
THE WHITE GAUNTLET.— *Just Published.*	do.	$1.50

A. S. Roe's Works.

A LONG LOOK AHEAD.—	A novel.	12mo. cloth, $1.50
TO LOVE AND TO BE LOVED.—	do.	do. $1.50
TIME AND TIDE.—	do.	do. $1.50
I'VE BEEN THINKING.—	do.	do. $1.50
THE STAR AND THE CLOUD.—	do.	do. $1.50
TRUE TO THE LAST.—	do.	do. $1.50
HOW COULD HE HELP IT?—	do.	do. $1.50
LIKE AND UNLIKE.—	do.	do. $1.50
LOOKING AROUND.—	do.	do. $1.50
WOMAN OUR ANGEL.—	do.	do. $1.50
THE CLOUD ON THE HEART.—*Just published.*	do.	$1.50

Richard B. Kimball.

WAS HE SUCCESSFUL?—	A novel.	12mo. cloth, $1.75
UNDERCURRENTS.—	do.	do. $1.75
SAINT LEGER.—	do.	do. $1.75
ROMANCE OF STUDENT LIFE.—do.	do.	$1.75
IN THE TROPICS.—	do.	do. $1.75
HENRY POWERS, Banker. do.	do.	$1.75
TO-DAY.—A novel. *Just published.*	do.	$1 75

Joseph Rodman Drake.

THE CULPRIT FAY.—A faery poem, with 100 illustrations. $2 00
    DO.   Superbly bound in turkey morocco. $5 00

"Brick" Pomeroy.

SENSE.—An illustrated vol. of fireside musings. 12mo. cl., $1 50
NONSENSE.— do. do. comic sketches. do. $1 50
OUR SATURDAY NIGHTS. do. pathos and sentiment. $1 50

Comic Books—Illustrated.

ARTEMUS WARD, His Book.—Letters, etc. 12mo. cl., $1 50
    DO.   His Travels—Mormons, etc. do. $1 50
    DO.   In London.—Punch Letters. do. $1 50
    DO.   His Panorama and Lecture. do. $1 50
    DO.   Sandwiches for Railroad. 25
JOSH BILLINGS ON ICE, and other things.— 12mo. cl., $1 50
    DO.   His Book of Proverbs, etc. do. $1 50
    DO.   Farmer's Allmanax. *Just published.* 25
FANNY FERN.—Folly as it Flies. $1 50
    DO.   Gingersnaps $1 50
VERDANT GREEN.—A racy English college story. 12mo. cl., $1 50
CONDENSED NOVELS, ETC.—By F. Bret Harte. do. $1.50
MILES O'REILLY.—His Book of Adventures. do. $1.50
ORPHEUS C. KERR.—Kerr Papers, 3 vols. do. $1.50
    DO.   Avery Glibun. A novel. $2.00
    DO.   Smoked Glass. 12mo. cl., $1.50

Children's Books—Illustrated.

THE ART OF AMUSING.—With 150 illustrations. 12mo. cl., $1.50
FRIENDLY COUNSEL FOR GIRLS.—A charming book. do. $1.50
THE CHRISTMAS FONT.—By Mary J. Holmes.   do. $1.00
ROBINSON CRUSOE—A Complete edition.   .   do. $1.50
LOUIE'S LAST TERM.—By author "Rutledge."   do. $1.75
ROUNDHEARTS, and other stories.—   do.   .   do. $1.75
PASTIMES WITH MY LITTLE FRIENDS.—   .   .   do. $1.50
WILL-O'-THE-WISP.—From the German.   .   do. $1.50

M. Michelet's Remarkable Works.

LOVE (L'AMOUR).—Translated from the French. 12mo. cl., $1.50
WOMAN (LA FEMME).—   .   do.   .   .   do. $1.50

Ernest Renan.

THE LIFE OF JESUS.—Translated from the French. 12mo.cl.$1.75
THE APOSTLES.—   .   .   do.   .   .   do. $1.75
SAINT PAUL.—   .   .   do.   .   .   do. $1.75

Popular Italian Novels.

DOCTOR ANTONIO.—A love story. By Ruffini 12mo. cl., $1.75
BEATRICE CENCI.—By Guerrazzi, with portrait   do. $1.75

Rev. John Cumming, D.D., of London.

THE GREAT TRIBULATION.—Two series.   12mo. cloth, $1.50
THE GREAT PREPARATION.—   do.   .   do. $1.50
THE GREAT CONSUMMATION.   do.   .   do. $1.50
THE LAST WARNING CRY.—   .   .   do. $1.50

Mrs. Ritchie (Anna Cora Mowatt).

FAIRY FINGERS.—A capital new novel   . 12mo. cloth, $1.75
THE MUTE SINGER.—   do.   .   do. $1.75
THE CLERGYMAN'S WIFE—and other stories.   do. $1.75

T. S. Arthur's New Works.

LIGHT ON SHADOWED PATHS.—A novel   12mo. cloth, $1.50
OUT IN THE WORLD.—   .   do.   .   .   do. $1.50

WHAT CAME AFTERWARDS.—   do.   .   .   do. $1.50
OUR NEIGHBORS.—   .   do.   .   .   do. $1.50

Geo. W. Carleton.

OUR ARTIST IN CUBA.—With 50 comic illustrations.   . $1.50
OUR ARTIST IN PERU.—   do.   do.   .   . $1.50
OUR ARTIST IN AFRICA.—(*In press*) do.   . $1.50

John Esten Cooke.

FAIRFAX.—   A brilliant new novel .   12mo. cloth, $1.50
HILT TO HILT.—   do.   .   .   .   do. $1.50
HAMMER AND RAPIER.— do.   .   .   .   do. $1.50
OUT OF THE FOAM.—   do.   *In press.*   do. $1.50

How to Make Money

AND HOW TO KEEP IT.—A practical, readable book, that ought to be in the hands of every person who wishes to earn money or to keep what he has. One of the best books ever published. By Thomas A. Davies.   12mo. cloth, $1.50

J. Cordy Jeaffreson.

A BOOK ABOUT LAWYERS.—A collection of interesting anecdotes and incidents connected with the most distinguished members of the Legal Profession.   .   12mo. cloth, $2.00

Fred. Saunders.

WOMAN, LOVE, AND MARRIAGE.—A charming volume about three most fascinating topics.   .   .   12mo. cloth, $1.50

Edmund Kirke.

AMONG THE PINES.—Or Life in the South. 12mo. cloth, $1.50
MY SOUTHERN FRIENDS.—   do.   .   .   do. $1.50
DOWN IN TENNESSEE.—   do.   .   .   do. $1.50
ADRIFT IN DIXIE.—   do.   .   .   do. $1.50
AMONG THE GUERILLAS.—   do.   .   .   do. $1.50

Charles Reade.

THE CLOISTER AND THE HEARTH.—A magnificent new novel—the best this author ever wrote.   .   8vo. cloth, $2.00

The Opera.

TALES FROM THE OPERAS.—A collection of clever stories, based upon the plots of all the famous operas. 12mo. cloth, $1.50

Robert B. Roosevelt.

THE GAME-FISH OF THE NORTH.—Illustrated. 12mo. cloth, $2.00
SUPERIOR FISHING.—   do.   do. $2.00
THE GAME-BIRDS OF THE NORTH.—   .   . do. $2.00

By the Author of "Rutledge."

RUTLEDGE.—A deeply interesting novel.   12mo. cloth, $1.75
THE SUTHERLANDS.—   do.   .   .   do.   . $1.75
FRANK WARRINGTON.—   do.   .   .   do.   . $1.75
ST. PHILIP'S.—   do.   .   .   do.   . $1.75
LOUIE'S LAST-TERM AT ST. MARY'S.—   .   do.   . $1.75
ROUNDHEARTS AND OTHER STORIES.—For children. do.   . $1.75
A ROSARY FOR LENT.—Devotional Readings.   do.   . $1.75

Love in Letters.

A collection of piquant love-letters.   .   12mo. cloth, $2.00

Dr. J. J. Craven.

THE PRISON-LIFE OF JEFFERSON DAVIS.—   .   12mo. cloth, $2.00

Walter Barrett, Clerk.

THE OLD MERCHANTS OF NEW YORK.—   Five vols. cloth, $10.

H. T. Sperry.

COUNTRY LOVE VS. CITY FLIRTATION.—   .   12mo. cloth, $2.00

Miscellaneous Works.

CHRIS AND OTHO.—A novel by Mrs. Julie P. Smith. . $1 75
CROWN JEWELS.—   do.   Mrs. Emma L. Moffett. $1 75
ADRIFT WITH A VENGEANCE.—   Kinahan Cornwallis. . $1.50
THE FRANCO-PRUSSIAN WAR IN 1870.—By W. D. Landon.
DREAM MUSIC.—Poems by Frederic Rowland Marvin. . $1.50
RAMBLES IN CUBA.—By an American Lady.   .   . $1.50
BEHIND THE SCENES, in the White House.—Keckley. . $2.00
YACHTMAN'S PRIMER.—For Amateur Sailors.—Warren.   50
RURAL ARCHITECTURE.—By M. Field. With illustrations. $2.00
TREATISE ON DEAFNESS.—By Dr. E. B. Lighthill. .   . $1.50
WOMEN AND THEATRES.—A new book, by Olive Logan. $1.50
WARWICK.—A new novel by Mansfield Tracy Walworth. $1.75
SIBYL HUNTINGTON.—A novel by Mrs. J. C. R. Dorr. . $1.75
LIVING WRITERS OF THE SOUTH.—By Prof. Davidson. . $2.00
STRANGE VISITORS.—A book from the Spirit World. . $1.50
UP BROADWAY, and its Sequel.—A story by Eleanor Kirk. $1.50
MILITARY RECORD, of Appointments in the U.S. Army. $5.00
HONOR BRIGHT.—A new American novel.   .   .   . $1.50
MALBROOK.—   do.   do.   do.   .   .   . $1.50
GUILTY OR NOT GUILTY.—   do.   do.   .   .   . $1.75
ROBERT GREATHOUSE.—A new novel by John F. Swift . $2.00
THE GOLDEN CROSS, and poems by Irving Van Wart, jr. $1.50
ATHALIAH.—A new novel by Joseph H. Greene, jr.   . $1.75
REGINA, and other poems.—By Eliza Cruger.   .   . $1.50
THE WICKEDEST WOMAN IN NEW YORK.—By C. H. Webb.   50
MONTALBAN.—A new American novel.   .   .   . $1.75
MADEMOISELLE MERQUEM.—A novel by George Sand. . $1.75
THE IMPENDING CRISIS OF THE SOUTH.—By H. R. Helper. $2.00
NOJOQUE—A Question for a Continent.—   do.   . $2.00
PARIS IN 1867.—By Henry Morford.   .   .   . $1.75
THE BISHOP'S SON.—A novel by Alice Cary.   .   . $1.75
CRUISE OF THE ALABAMA AND SUMTER.—By Capt. Semmes. $1.50
HELEN COURTENAY.—A novel, author "Vernon Grove." $1.75
SOUVENIRS OF TRAVEL.—By Madame Octavia W. LeVert. $2.00
VANQUISHED.—A novel by Agnes Leonard.   .   . $1.75
WILL-O'-THE-WISP.—A child's book, from the German . $1.50
FOUR OAKS.—A novel by Kamba Thorpe.   .   . $1.75
THE CHRISTMAS FONT.—A child's book, by M. J. Holmes. $1 00
POEMS, BY SARAH T. BOLTON. $1.50
MARY BRANDEGEE—A novel by Cuyler Pine.   .   . $1.75
RENSHAWE.—   do.   do.   .   .   . $1.75
MOUNT CALVARY.—By Matthew Hale Smith.   .   . $2.00
PROMETHEUS IN ATLANTIS.—A prophecy.   .   .   . $2.00
TITAN AGONISTES.—An American novel.   .   .   . $2 00